Portraits of Contemporary African Americans

by
Doris Hunter Metcalf

illustrated by Paul Manktelow

Cover by Paul Manktelow

Copyright © 1993, Good Apple

ISBN No. 0-86653-723-6

Printing No. 9876

Good Apple
23740 Hawthorne Blvd.
Torrance, CA 90505

Table of Contents

GA1442

GA1442

Dedication

This book is dedicated to my parents
James and Bessie Hunter
For their love and inspiration
and
In memory of Mrs. Edith Pride
For the same reasons

Introduction

Portraits of Contemporary African Americans is a social studies resource activity book. It is designed to supplement textbooks and other social studies programs in presenting the achievements of contemporary African Americans.

The book consists of a personal data section and a biographical information section followed by activity sheets that develop and enhance creative thinking skills, reading and comprehension skills, and writing and research skills. The personal data section serves as a quick source of reference. It includes such information as birth year, birthplace, field of endeavor, occupation, and awards and achievements, along with a sketch of the individual.

The biographical section gives more in-depth information about the life of the individual. An information update sheet in the back of the book can be used after each unit. It provides the opportunity for students to update information on each individual. Word searches on the last pages of the book provide useful learning activities for students who finish class work early or as activities in a learning center.

Because it explores the contributions and achievements of contemporary African Americans, this book can lead students to a greater awareness of the contributions of this group of people. It can also lead to a better understanding between African Americans and other students, and it can help build self-confidence and self-esteem among African American students.

Through the information and activities presented in this book, students will discover that hard work and commitment are the keys to success and that the future belongs to those who prepare themselves for it.

The contemporary African Americans who are highlighted are Bill Cosby, Colin Powell, Oprah Winfrey, Michael Jordan, Arsenio Hall, Carl Lewis, Douglas Wilder, Michael Jackson, Coretta Scott King, Rosa Parks, Stevie Wonder, Marva Collins, George Carruthers, Wynton Marsalis, Eldrick Woods, Spike Lee, Mae Jemison, Florence Griffith Joyner, Charlayne Hunter-Gault, and Bryant Gumbel.

GA1442

Personal Data

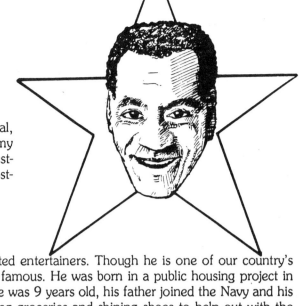

Name: Bill Cosby (William Henry Cosby)
Birth Year: 1937
Birthplace: Philadelphia, Pennsylvania
Fields: Entertainment and education
Occupations: Comedian, educator, and author
Awards and Achievements: 1985 Spingarn Medal, NAACP Image Award, numerous Emmy and Grammy awards for acting and recording, author of several best-selling books. *The Cosby Show* became one of the most-watched TV shows in the United States.

Biographical Information

Bill Cosby is one of America's most loved and respected entertainers. Though he is one of our country's most popular celebrities, Bill Cosby was not always so famous. He was born in a public housing project in the poor Germantown district of Philadelphia. When he was 9 years old, his father joined the Navy and his mother went to work as a maid. Bill got a job delivering groceries and shining shoes to help out with the family income. When Bill went to high school, he became a star athlete, but he clowned around and did not take his subjects seriously. As a result, he had to repeat the tenth grade. Bill Cosby was disappointed that he had failed his schoolwork, so he dropped out of school and got a job as a shoe repairman. He soon grew tired and bored with his job and joined the Navy. He learned that there aren't many interesting jobs for a person without a good education. While serving in the Navy, Bill Cosby grew up to be a serious, young man. He completed high school and went on to college. This time he earned good grades in his classes and excelled in sports too. He found that if a person tries hard enough, he can be good at more than one thing.

One summer while he was in college, he worked as a bartender and told jokes and stories as he worked. The people liked his jokes and stories so much that the owner offered him a job as a comedian. More people began coming to hear his jokes and stories. Bill Cosby had learned another valuable lesson. He had learned that clowning around could pay off when it is done at the right time and in the right place.

Before long, Bill began to receive offers from many other places. He had a big decision to make: Should he quit college and become a full-time comedian or continue with his college studies? He finally decided to continue his studies. Later, when he became a full-time comedian, he began receiving even more job offers than before, and more money. In 1964 his first big break came when he was offered a role in a television program called *I Spy*. He accepted the role and his career took off like a rocket. He starred in award-winning TV shows, acted in several successful movies, made many best-selling comedy records and wrote several best-selling books.

Bill Cosby also went back to college and earned his doctorate degree.

Bill Cosby used his expertise in education to teach young children across the nation by starring in such educational TV programs as *Sesame Street* and the *Electric Company*. His Saturday morning cartoon show, *Fat Albert and the Cosby Kids,* entertained and taught children important lessons in life. His popular TV show *The Cosby Show* entertained and taught family members to love and respect one another. In addition to acting and teaching, Bill Cosby has also starred in television commercials. Perhaps you have seen him in ads for pudding or film.

As busy as he is, he still finds time for his family. He believes that a good education is very important; and to help this become a reality for needy students, he donates both time and money to colleges across the United States.

When Bill Cosby was growing up, there were three things that he wanted to accomplish in life. He wanted a good education, he wanted to be a successful actor, and he wanted to make people laugh. He has succeeded in all three areas. Bill Cosby is a superstar.

GA1442

The Spingarn

In 1985, Bill Cosby won the NAACP Spingarn Medal for his achievement in the fields of entertainment and education. The Spingarn is a gold medal awarded to African Americans who have reached the highest achievement in their fields in the previous year or over a period of years. The medal has a figure of justice engraved on the front. The winner's name and the date on which the award is given is engraved on the back.

Listed below are some categories in which the Spingarn Medal has been given. Use the world almanac, encyclopedia and other reference books to list as many winners as you can for each category.

Science	Education	Sports

Government	Business	Leadership

Art	Arts/Entertainment

Select one person from each category and explain why each person was awarded the Spingarn.

2

Bill's Book

Bill Cosby wrote a best-selling book called *Fatherhood*. This book highlights in a humorous way some of the problems of being a father in today's world.

Imagine that you have signed a contract to write a book called *Childhood*. Your book will be about the problems of being a child in today's world. Write the introduction to your book on the book page below. Tell what problems you will write about. When you are finished, compare the problems that you wrote about with those of your classmates. Are some of the problems the same? Are some different? Make a class list and discuss your conclusions.

On the back, design a cover for your book.

3

GA1442

Should I?

Every day of your life you have to make decisions. Should I wear the red shirt, or should I wear the blue shirt? Should I go to the dance, or should I stay home? Should I do my report today or tomorrow?

Many decisions are not easy to make. Most often they are difficult. Many times they involve risk or some kind of consequence.

One day Bill Cosby had to make a difficult decision. He had to decide if he wanted to continue his college education or drop out and become a full-time comedian. He dropped out of college and became a very successful comedian. All decisions do not turn out quite as well.

What About Some of Your Decisions?

Complete the chart showing five decisions that you have made and the results of each. Bill Cosby's decision is used as an example.

The Decision	What I Decided	Results
Example: To quit college and become a full-time comedian	To quit college	A successful comedian and educator
1.		
2.		
3.		
4.		
5.		

What is one of the worst decisions that you have ever made?_____

_____

What is one of the best decisions that you have ever made? _____

_____

Let's Face It

Bill Cosby became famous by using stories from his childhood which he changed to make them humorous. He also made his stories humorous by changing his facial expressions and by using his voice to give his stories sound effects.

Cut out the face parts below and paste them together on a sheet of paper to make five different faces. Make each face show a different mood. Give a descriptive name to each face that you create.

Example: Moody Mandy

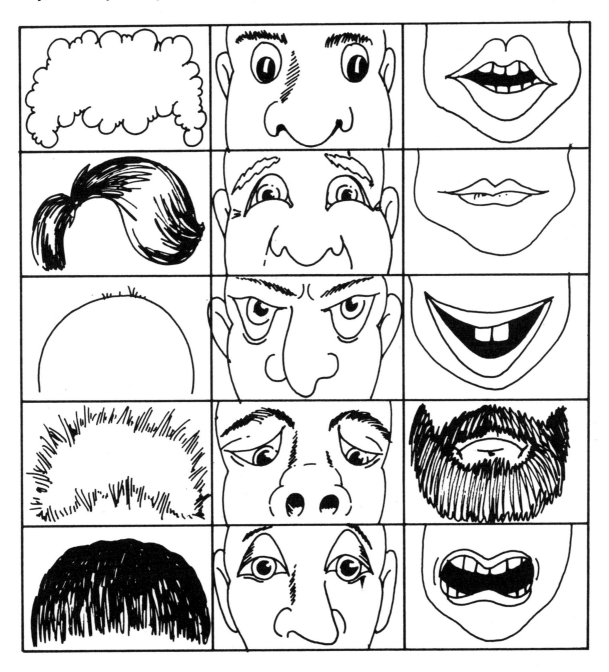

GA1442

Father! Father!

On Bill Cosby's television show, he played the father of five children. What are five things that you think all fathers should know about raising children?

1. _____
2. _____
3. _____
4. _____
5. _____

Father's Day is celebrated the third Sunday in June. On that day fathers often get gifts or cards from their families. Design a Father's Day card for your father or for someone who is like a father to you.

Front of Card   Inside of Card

On the back of this page, create a medal to be awarded to someone you would nominate as Father of the Year.

Personal Data

Name: Colin Powell
Birth Year: 1937
Birthplace: Harlem, New York City
Field: Military
Occupation: Chairman, Joint Chiefs of Staff
Awards and Achievements: White House Fellow; National Security Advisor under President Ronald Reagan; Presidential Medal of Freedom July, 1991; NAACP Spingarn Medal, 1991; numerous civic and social awards; military decorations, including two Purple Hearts, a Bronze Star, the Soldier's Medal, the Legion of Merit and the Distinguished Service Award

Biographical Information

Top brass, *top gun*, *top flight*, and *top-notch* are all words used to describe this United States' top military man. His real name is Colin Luther Powell, and he is Chairman of the Joint Chiefs of Staff. He is the youngest officer ever to hold this position and the first African American to hold America's highest military post. Colin Powell was only fifty-two years old in 1989 when he was appointed to this position by President George Bush.

As Joint Chiefs of Staff Chairman, he is the chief military advisor to the President. As Chief Military Advisor, Colin Powell has the job of making sure that the United States is prepared to go to war and win if a war should become necessary. Colin Powell did not become America's greatest military advisor overnight. He has been an army officer for more than thirty years and has climbed the ladder of success step-by-step.

He was born in Harlem and raised in the South Bronx area. His father was a shipping clerk, and his mother was a seamstress. He grew up in the midst of poverty, drugs and street violence, but through the efforts of his mother and father, Colin Powell managed to survive and escape the ghetto environment. He graduated from high school and went to City College in New York. Afterwards, he joined the army. During his military career he was awarded several medals and decorations. At each step along the way, Colin Powell prepared himself by becoming the best that he could be. When the word came that he was to be appointed to the nation's highest military post, he knew that his reward had come and that his preparation had paid off.

When the United States went to war against Iraq in January 1991, Chief Military Advisor Colin Powell organized the fastest large-scale deployment of U.S. troops in the history of the United States. Within forty-three days the United States had won the war, and Colin Powell had become a hero to millions of people around the world.

When Colin Powell's term as Chairman of the Joint Chiefs of Staff ended in May of 1991, President George Bush reappointed him to continue to serve in that position for another two years.

On July 3, 1991, Colin Powell was again honored. He received one of the most prestigious awards of all. President George Bush presented him with the Medal of Freedom Award for his leadership during the Persian Gulf War.

Major Powell credits his climb to success to the inspiration that he got from other African American military men before him who helped to open the doors of opportunity. No one knows for sure what Colin Powell will do next. But it is already known that his climb to success has inspired millions of young people in America to prepare and educate themselves for full and productive lives.

GA1442

Tough Decisions

Every person in the world is faced with tough decisions at one time or another in his or her life. As Chairman of the Joint Chiefs of Staff, Colin Powell has to make many tough decisions. One of the toughest decisions is that of military defense spending. He has to decide how best to spend billions of dollars for the defense and welfare of the United States.

You are a governmental advisor, and your job is to determine how to spend $15 billion. There are some strings attached. You must spend the money in billion dollar lump sums, and you can spend it only on the following areas. Indicate how many billion dollars you would spend on each area.

Cleaning up the environment _____   AIDS research _____

Exploring space and planets _____   Food for the hungry _____

Homes for the homeless _____   Medical care for the elderly _____

Cancer research _____   Homes for abused children _____

Treatment centers for alcoholics _____   Help to find missing children _____

Training people for new jobs _____   Treatment centers for drug addicts _____

What's Your Decision?

1. You want to be a medical doctor, but you do not have the $100,000 to attend medical school. You have two choices. You can borrow the money and pay it back after you graduate and get a job, or you can agree to work at a low salary in a low income area as a doctor for five years and the government will pay all of your medical expenses. Which will you choose? Give reasons for your choice.

   _____

   _____

   _____

   _____

2. Your parent has received a job promotion to become supervisor with more money and more prestige. There is a problem. The new job requires that your parent move to another state, and you and the family would have to move too. You're a senior in high school, and you are looking forward to getting a scholarship from your school at the end of the year. If you move, you cannot get the scholarship. In addition, the move will take you away from your friends and relatives. Your parent leaves the choice up to you. What will you choose to do? Be sure to consider other members of the family in your decision. Give reasons for your choice.

   _____

   _____

   _____

   _____

Coins, Coins, Coins

Take a coin from your pocket or borrow one from your teacher. Observe the coin. Notice the words, pictures or symbols that are inscribed on the coin. The United States has honored several famous Americans by issuing coins in their honor.

You are in charge of issuing a coin to honor General Colin Powell. Complete the coin design below to show how a Colin Powell coin might look.

Coin collecting is one of the most popular hobbies in the world. Use the library to find out more about coins and coin collecting. Write your information in the space below.

_____

_____

_____

_____

_____

In 1950 a commemorative half dollar coin was issued to honor the famous African American Booker T. Washington. Research and write an informational paragraph on his life and achievements.

_____

_____

_____

_____

_____

_____

_____

_____

_____

GA1442

Stress Management

Major Colin Powell has a very important job with a very busy schedule. Such a job can create a lot of stress.

It has been found that exercise, relaxation, and fun activities can help reduce stress. When Major Powell has a few extra hours of free time, he relaxes by rebuilding old Volvo cars.

Imagine that you are manager of Stress Control International, a stress management company that schedules relaxing programs for busy executives. Your company has designed and built a portable traveling recreational vehicle that can be driven to a busy executive's office or home. What exercise and recreation equipment will you include in your vehicle? Draw a picture of the inside of your portable traveling recreational vehicle.

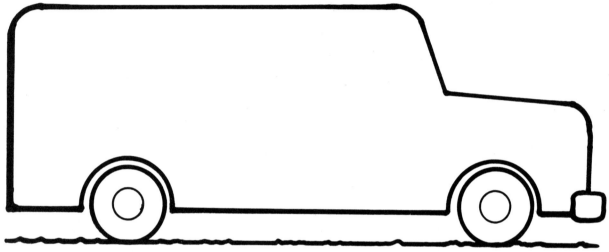

In the space below create the front of a brochure that advertises your Stress Management Program. It will be sent to Major Powell. Be creative and make your brochure cover as attractive as possible.

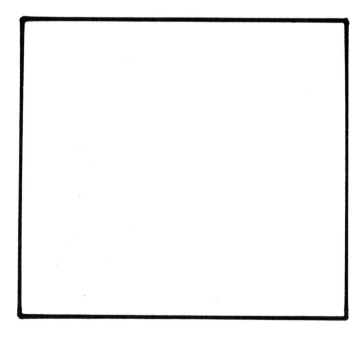

GA1442

Our Speaker Today . . .

You are the president of an international civic club. The club has invited Major Colin Powell to speak at its annual patriotism luncheon. As president of the club you will be responsible for introducing the speaker.

Write your introduction speech in the space below. Include information from the story and any other reference books.

Ladies and gentlemen, may I have your attention . . . _____

_____

_____

_____

_____

_____

Make a list of the important people in your town and city that will be invited to the luncheon.

Guest List

1. _____	5. _____	9. _____
2. _____	6. _____	10. _____
3. _____	7. _____	11. _____
4. _____	8. _____	12. _____

In the space below, design an invitation to be sent to each guest.

Front of Invitation   Inside of Invitation

GA1442

I.S. 52

In 1991 Colin Powell returned to Inner-City School 52 in the Bronx, New York, (his old junior high school) to speak to the students. His advice to the students was to stay in school and get a good education. He urged them not to let drugs, violence and gangs ruin their lives and shatter their dreams of becoming successful. He had grown up in the same neighborhood as they, and he did not let the situation defeat him because he was determined to make something of himself.

The time is in the future. You have become a famous person, and you have returned to your junior high school to talk to the students. What have you become? Write a speech telling all about your success and how you worked to get where you are. Encourage the students to strive for excellence.

Suppose the following outstanding African Americans could have visited your junior high school classroom. Complete the statements telling what each might have talked about. Use information from the encyclopedia if you need to.

1. George Washington Carver once visited my classroom. He told the class about_____

   _____

2. Daniel Hale Williams once visited my classroom. He told the class about _____

   _____

3. Harriet Tubman once visited my classroom. She told the class about the time that she

   _____

4. Dr. Martin Luther King, Jr., once visited my classroom. He told the class about _____

   _____

5. Garrett Morgan once visited my classroom. He told the class about_____

   _____

6. Thurgood Marshall once visited my classroom. He told the class that _____

   _____

7. Arsenio Hall once visited my classroom. He told the class a joke about_____

   _____

8. Michael Jordan once visited my classroom. He told the class that _____

   _____

9. Alex Haley once visited my classroom. He told the class about_____

   _____

10. Michael Jackson once visited my classroom. He told the class this about his new video.

    _____

Personal Data

Name: Michael Jeffrey Jordan
Birth Year: 1963
Birthplace: Brooklyn, New York
Field: Sports
Occupation: Professional basketball player
Awards and Achievements: 1989 *World Almanac* top hero; 1990 *World Almanac* top hero; 1990-1991 top hero in sports; NBA Rookie of the Year, 1984-1985; led the U.S. men's basketball team to win a gold medal in the 1984 Summer Olympic Games; 1987 and 1988 NBA Most Valuable Player; June 12, 1991, led the Chicago Bulls to win the National Basketball Association Championship for the first time ever; College Player of the Year, 1987-1988; All-Star Slam Dunk Champion; 1992, led the Chicago Bulls to their second NBA Championship and named Most Valuable Player of the NBA

Biographical Information

Some people say that it is his spectacular shooting that has made him famous. Others say that it is his acrobatic jump-and-dunk shot. Still others say that it is a combination of these things. But one thing that everyone agrees on is the fact that Michael Jordan is one of the most exciting basketball players in the world.

Like many other famous athletes before him, Michael Jordan did not become a success overnight. His success has taken years of practice, hard work and self-discipline. Michael knew that he wanted to become a great basketball player, so he set his sight on his goal and worked hard to achieve it.

Michael Jeffrey Jordan was born in Brooklyn, New York, and grew up in Wilmington, North Carolina. Neither his father nor his mother was good in sports. At first Michael was not good in sports either. In fact, he was cut from his high school basketball team when he was in the tenth grade. During the summer before his eleventh grade year, Michael grew from 5' 11" to 6' 3". He found that with his increase in height he could outplay any of his classmates and friends. He quickly became interested in playing basketball. During this time, he played mostly to amaze his friends. Little did he know that he was perfecting his shots and moves to make himself one of the world's most exciting basketball players.

When Michael finished high school, most of the best college basketball teams in the country wanted him to play with them; but Michael chose the University of North Carolina. In 1982 he led the university Tar Heels to the college basketball championship. During his second and third years in college, he was chosen College Basketball Player of the Year. In the 1984 Summer Olympics, he led his team to win the gold medal in men's basketball.

Afterwards Michael Jordan became the hero of just about every basketball fan in the world. His skills have led him to become one of the most watched players in the history of basketball. They have brought him fortune, fame and fans. Even though Michael Jordan is a famous person, he still takes time to care. When he is not on the court playing basketball, he can often be found donating money to his favorite charity, signing autographs for starry-eyed fans and visiting sick children in homes and hospitals.

GA1442

Invent a Game

Basketball is one of the most widely played and watched games in the world. Football is another favorite sport around the world. Just for fun, can you combine the two games to invent a new game? Use the space below to design a field or court on which the game will be played. Sketch a design of the ball that will be used and write some game rules in the rule book below.

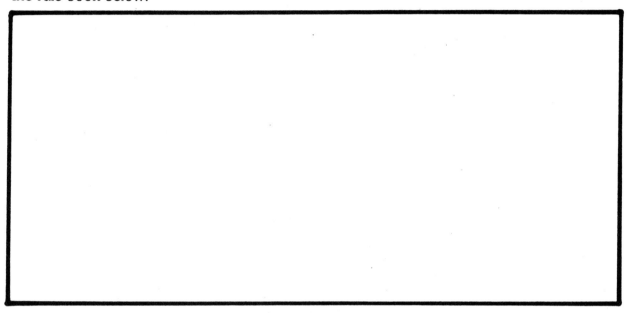

Field or Court

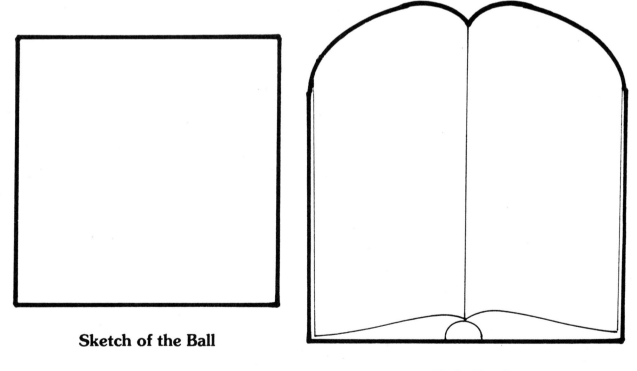

Sketch of the Ball

Rule Book

14

GA1442

Just Suppose

Michael Jordan has not only gained fortune and fame playing professional basketball, he has also become famous for his television commercials. His fast foods, breakfast cereal, soft drink and athletic shoe commercials are among television's most familiar ones.

Just suppose that the Do-More Athletic Shoe Company has asked you to design a new type of athletic shoe for Michael Jordan to advertise. Make a sketch of your new athletic shoe and write an advertisement telling all about the new shoe and why the new shoe is better than any other.

Name of New Athletic Shoe

_____

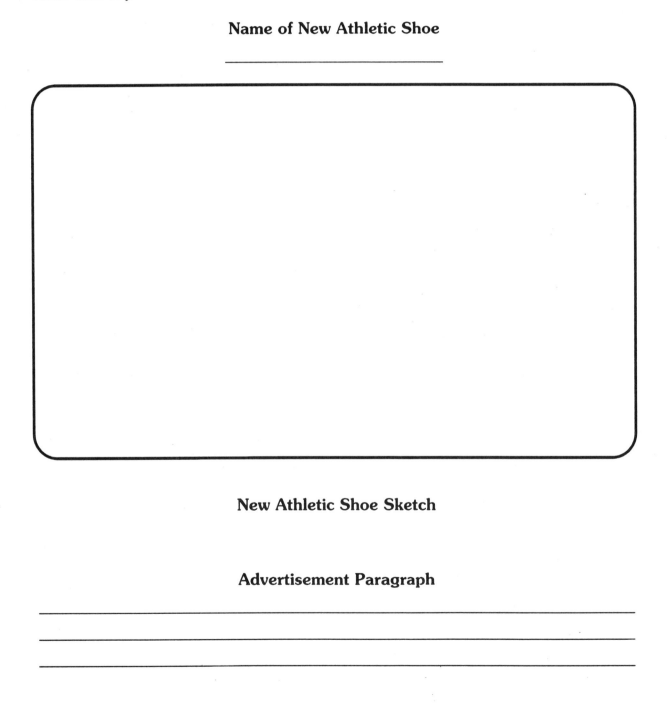

New Athletic Shoe Sketch

Advertisement Paragraph

_____

_____

_____

GA1442

Too Tall

When Michael Jordan stands beside people of average height, he towers over them. Most children want to grow up to be tall, but as Michael Jordan can tell you, being tall has its disadvantages. Many tall people find that most things, especially furniture, are too short for their long arms and legs. Beds are too short; chairs and tables are too low. They have to remember to duck their heads when passing through doorways. What are some other disadvantages of being tall? Make a list.

1. _____   5. _____   8. _____

2. _____   6. _____   9. _____

3. _____   7. _____   10. _____

4. _____

When you are finished, make a list of advantages of being tall. Discuss your list with a classmate's list, then with the whole class.

1. _____   5. _____   8. _____

2. _____   6. _____   9. _____

3. _____   7. _____   10. _____

4. _____

How many different disadvantages did the entire class list? How many different advantages did they list? Make a chart of the class results.

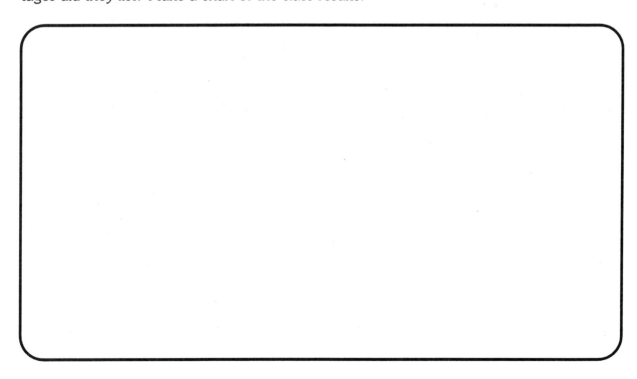

GA1442

My Hero Spiral

A hero is often defined as "one who is admired by others." Most people have heroes. Some heroes are imaginary and some are real. Michael Jordan is a hero to many people. He has been selected as top hero and sports hero for the *World Almanac's* Hero of Young America survey for more than three years. Who are your heroes?

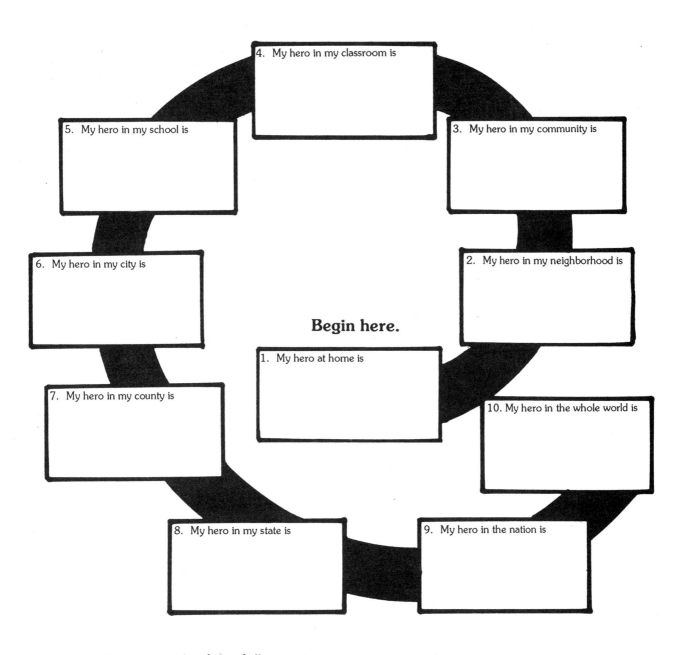

4. My hero in my classroom is

5. My hero in my school is

3. My hero in my community is

6. My hero in my city is

2. My hero in my neighborhood is

Begin here.

1. My hero at home is

7. My hero in my county is

10. My hero in the whole world is

8. My hero in my state is

9. My hero in the nation is

List your hero in each of the following areas:

Sports _____   Movie _____

Singer _____   Television _____

Imaginary Hero _____

Michael Jordan's Road to Success

Cut out the success squares and paste them in sequential order on Michael Jordan's Road to Success.

Success Squares

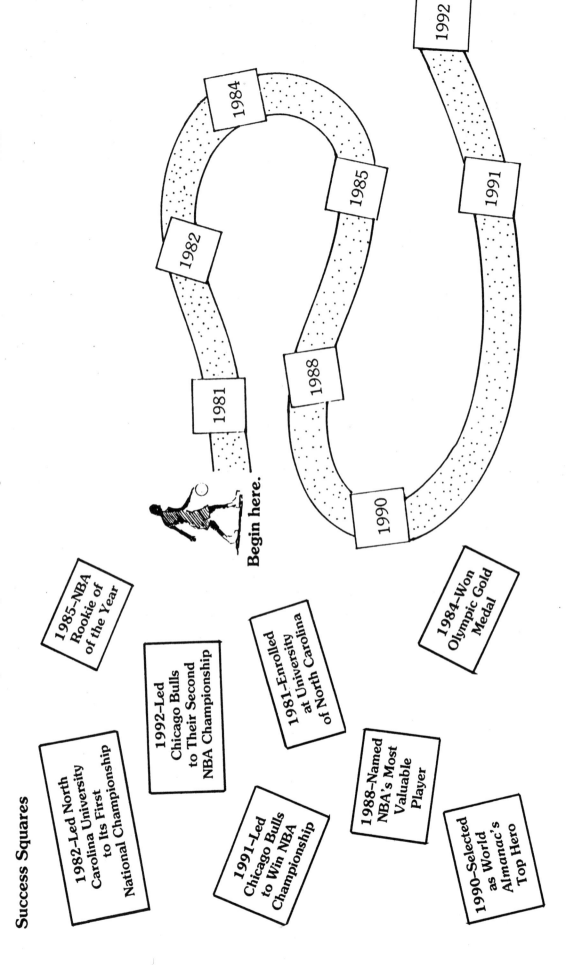

Personal Data

Name: Mae Jemison
Birthplace: Chicago, Illinois
Fields: Science and medicine
Occupation: Astronaut
Awards and Achievements: First African American astronaut

Biographical Information

"We choose to go to the moon in this decade, not because it is easy but because it is hard, because that goal will serve to organize and measure the best of our energies and skills; because that challenge is one that we are willing to accept, and one which we intend to win."

Those words were spoken by President John F. Kennedy when he spoke to the American people challenging them to be the first country to put a man on the moon. The American people answered the challenge, and on July 19, 1969, two American astronauts landed on the moon. The nation was pleasantly shocked and surprised. Newspapers and television stations across the nation carried the headlines. In Chicago, Illinois, a thirteen-year-old girl watched the evening news. She was fascinated by the broadcast. She had always been interested in space. "That's what I want to do someday," she thought.

That little girl's name was Mae Jemison. Mae was one of three children born to Charlie and Dorothy Jemison. When she was growing up she loved science. Her parents supported and encouraged her interest in science. At the age of sixteen, when most students are in the tenth grade, Mae was graduating from high school. When she finished high school, she went to college and earned a B.S. degree in chemical engineering. After her college graduation, she went to medical school and became a doctor. Then she worked with the Peace Corps in Africa. In 1985 she returned to the United States and practiced medicine in Los Angeles. Through all of her education and work, Mae's interest in space science never left. A friend of Mae's learned of her interest in space and encouraged Mae to apply for admission to NASA's astronaut training program. Mae followed her friend's advice and filled out an application. When the time came for the selection of astronauts, Mae was one of fifteen chosen out of a field of nearly 2000 applicants. A part of Mae's dream had come true. She became an astronaut trainee and trained as a mission specialist. A mission specialist does experiments in space, helps launch satellites into orbit and may perform walks in space.

Dr. Mae Jemison looks forward to the day when her entire dream can be fulfilled. That complete fulfillment of performing her duties aboard a spacecraft is scheduled for sometime in the near future. Until that day Dr. Mae Jemison will continue to train and prepare so that when the opportunity comes along, she will be ready. She has already made history by becoming the first African American woman mission specialist. Now she is set to become another first–the first African American woman in space.

Daydream

When Mae Jemison was a small child, she dreamed of becoming an astronaut. In the later years, she daydreamed about being strapped into a seat aboard a space shuttle poised on the launch pad ready for lift-off! In the space below write a diary entry for Mae on the day before the launch.

_____

_____

_____

_____

_____

_____

_____

_____

What do you dream of becoming when you grow up? Write about it.

_____

_____

_____

_____

_____

_____

_____

_____

_____

_____

GA1442

Space Doodles

In addition to formal training, astronauts have to be able to think creatively. They have to be able to see things in a different way. How creative are you?

Show your creativity by turning each of these drawings into something related to space.

In the space at the bottom of the square, tell about each drawing.

Make nine doodles of your own on the back of this sheet. Ask a friend to turn each doodle into a space-related object.

GA1442

Space Shuttle Insignia

Members of a space shuttle crew usually wear blue flight suits with a space patch or insignia on the arm or left shoulder. Below is a picture of the space insignia worn by the astronauts of the *Challenger* crew who were killed in a 1986 space shuttle explosion.

Draw your own space shuttle insignia or patch with you and six of your classmates as crew members.

GA1442

Blast Off!

Congratulations! You have been selected from among thousands of applicants to become one of the crew members for an early fall space shuttle flight. However, before you leave, you must complete the following activities. After finishing each activity, color the corresponding section of the rocket. When you have colored every section, you are ready to blast off. Bon voyage!

Use a dictionary and/or an encyclopedia if you need help in completing the activities.

1. Make a list of five compound words that begin with the word *space*.
   Example: spacesuit
2. Research and write a paragraph on the Marshal Space Flight Center in Huntsville, Alabama, and its role in the space program.
3. Find out what the letters *NASA* stand for.
4. Write a poem about space.
5. Write a space-related word for each letter in the word *astronaut*.
6. The first astronaut on the moon said, "That's one small step for man, one giant leap for mankind." Write a sentence for the first man who arrives on Mars.
7. What is a Russian astronaut called?
8. Should we spend more or less on space exploration? Take a stand and write a paragraph to support your answer.
9. List five advantages and five disadvantages of zero gravity or weightlessness.
10. Write definitions of the following words for a first grader:

   a. star _____

   _____

   b. planet _____

   _____

   c. astronaut _____

   _____

   d. cosmonaut _____

   _____

   e. solar system _____

   _____

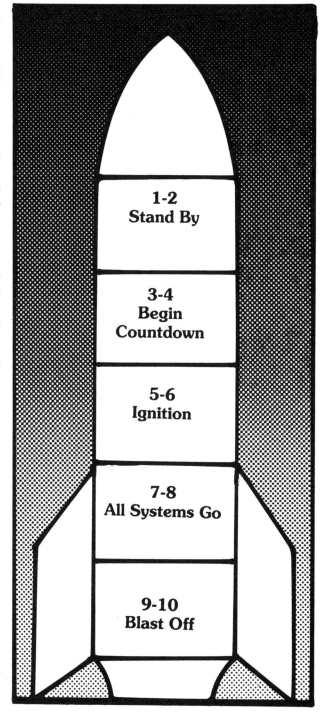

1-2
Stand By

3-4
Begin
Countdown

5-6
Ignition

7-8
All Systems Go

9-10
Blast Off

Luxury Space Cruises, Inc.

The year is 3025. You are the proud owner of the *Luxury Space Cruise* spaceship. Draw a picture of the spaceship. Label to show the different areas for eating, sleeping, etc.

Write a radio and/or television ad to advertise cruise ship trips.

Write an advertisement for the cruise on the billboard below.

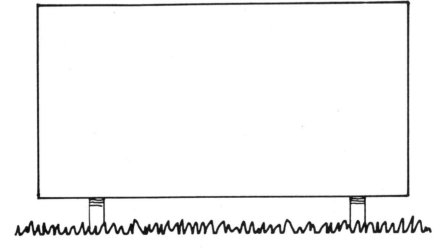

Design a ticket for the cruise.

Personal Data

Name: Arsenio Hall
Birth Year: 1955
Birthplace: Cleveland, Ohio
Field: Entertainment
Occupations: Comedian and actor
Awards and Achievements: American Comedy Award. *The Arsenio Hall Show* was nominated for three Emmy awards.

Biographical Information

It is late at night, the band blares, the announcer wails. A tall, skinny man with large teeth gives a grand smile. He drops to his knees for a few moments of silent prayer. Within seconds he takes his place on stage. He raises a clenched fist and rotates it in a circle. The audience responds with a barking chant "Woof! Woof! Woof," and one of television's best late night talk shows is under way. The tall, skinny man is Arsenio Hall. It has been a long, hard pull, but Arsenio has finally made it. He has become a famous talk show host, the first contemporary African American to do so. As a boy growing up in a Cleveland ghetto, he had dreamed of becoming a famous talk show host. When he was nine years old, Arsenio would set up chairs in his basement. The empty chairs would be his audience, and he would pretend to be Johnny Carson. At times, he would invite neighborhood children to be interviewed on his make-believe late night show. If you knew about Arsenio Hall's background you might be surprised at his accomplishments. In 1955, Arsenio was born to Reverend Fred Hall and his wife Annie in a Cleveland, Ohio, ghetto. They named their little son Arsenio. When Arsenio was five years old something happened to him that gave him an overwhelming desire to leave the ghetto. A rat ran across his foot!

At the age of seven, Arsenio became interested in magic. He spent all of his free time practicing magic tricks. When he was good enough, he performed at birthday parties, talent shows and wedding receptions. During his teen years, Arsenio played drums in his high school marching band. He became the class clown, entertaining his classmates with his jokes and stories. One day when he was a high school senior, a famous comedian visited his school. Arsenio liked the comedian and his act, and he liked the way the audience responded to the comedian with bursts of laughter and applause. It was then that he decided that he wanted to become a stand-up comedian. Following his graduation from high school, Arsenio enrolled in college and graduated with a degree in speech. Arsenio then moved to Chicago with his mother, and began performing in some of the local nightclubs. At Christmas 1979 his big break came. He impressed a famous singer who financed his move to Los Angeles where opportunities for young comedians were more plentiful. In Los Angeles he became a frequent guest on *The Tonight Show,* the one that he had imitated and watched for many years. In July 1984 Arsenio was selected to cohost a music variety show, *Solid Gold.* In 1988 Arsenio's career took a different turn. He starred in his first movie. It was called *Coming to America.* By the end of June 1988, the movie earned one of the highest totals in Hollywood history.

In August 1988, when his movie was still drawing large crowds at the box office, Arsenio was asked to host a one-hour late night talk show. Arsenio was excited. His long awaited dream of being the host of his own TV show had come true. When *The Arsenio Hall Show* began on January 3, 1989, it became an overwhelming success within eight months. In May 1989 he was named funniest supporting actor for his role in *Coming to America.* Two months later, *The Arsenio Hall Show* was nominated for three Emmy awards. In its first few months on the air the show yielded unexpectedly high TV ratings. In November 1989, Arsenio Hall's second movie was released; it was called *Harlem Nights.* Arsenio Hall believes that in today's world of stress, laughter is important therapy. He believes that relaxation is just as important as a job. Arsenio relaxes by spending time with his two close comedian friends Eddie Murphy and Richard Pryor. He also likes to play basketball. He strongly disapproves of using drugs, and he appears often in television commercials telling people about the horrors of drug addition.

Hold Fast to Dreams

When Arsenio announced that he wanted to become a famous comedian, he was warned that it couldn't be done. He was told that children who grow up in the ghetto do not become famous people, only famous criminals. Despite discouragements like these, Arsenio continued to hold fast to his dreams and to work to make his dreams come true. Many young people who have dreams are often discouraged by those who do not believe in them.

Write some encouraging remarks on the bumper stickers below to encourage people to hold on to their dreams. Use your best writing and drawing. Use crayons or markers to make your work more attractive.

Example: Keep your dream afloat.

A couplet is a poem of two lines that rhyme. Write a couplet about dreams.

Example: Dreams are neat.
            They do not repeat.

GA1442

Only the Lonely

Arsenio had a lonely and disjointed childhood. He was an only child, and when he was five years old, his mother and father divorced. Arsenio and his mother moved in with his grandmother. After the move Arsenio continued to see his father, but his father's job did not permit him to spend much time with Arsenio. Arsenio had few friends. He spent most of his time alone practicing magic tricks and watching *The Tonight Show*. His teachers wrote on his report card that he needed more attention at home. His Sunday School teacher said that his mind always seemed to be on something else far away.

Almost every person has felt lonely at one time or another. In the space below tell about a time that you felt lonely.

Use your senses and imagination to describe loneliness.

Loneliness is _____.
                                  (color)

It tastes like _____.

It feels like _____.

It sounds like _____.

It looks like this (draw a picture or symbol).

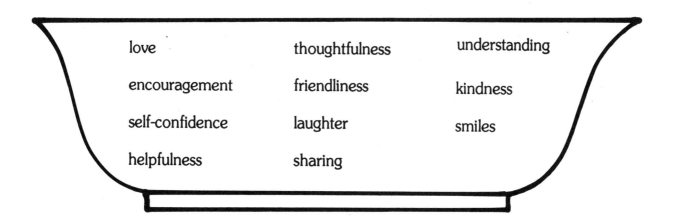

love   thoughtfulness   understanding

encouragement   friendliness   kindness

self-confidence   laughter   smiles

helpfulness   sharing

Use words from the mixing bowl to write a recipe to overcome loneliness.

Recipe to Overcome Loneliness

In a large bowl combine 1 cup of _____

Sprinkle with 1 teaspoon of _____

Toss with 1 cup of _____

Add $1/2$ cup of _____

Arsenio Acrostic

In an acrostic poem, the first letters of the lines spell a word reading down.
Example:

> **D**oing Things
>
> **A**nd
>
> **D**oing them right

Make an acrostic poem from the letters in *Arsenio*. Remember that the lines can be any length, and they don't have to rhyme.

A

R

S

E

N

I

O

Can you make an acrostic from the letters in Arsenio's last name? Try it. You might consider using words from Arsenio's biographical information.

H

A

L

L

Now write your first name vertically on a sheet of paper and make an acrostic from the letters. Can you do your last name? Try it.

Arsenio's Joke Book

When Arsenio became a comedian, he wrote down his jokes and stories in a notebook. Add some of your own original, funny jokes and stories to Arsenio's notebook pages below.

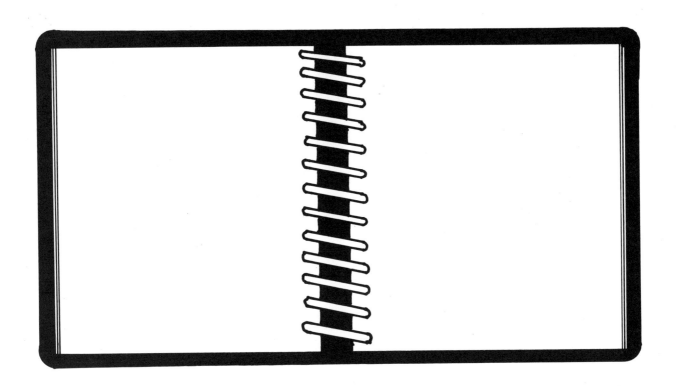

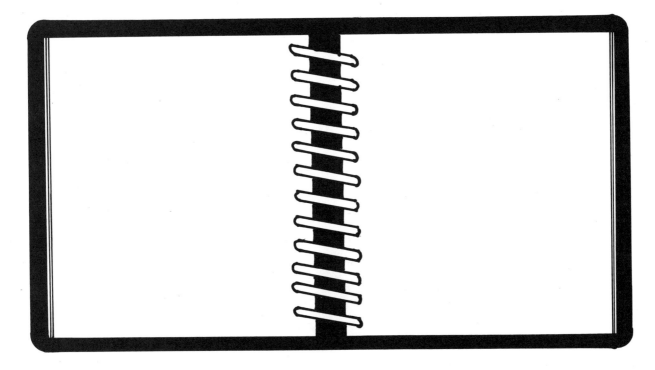

GA1442

Serious Arsenio

Arsenio Hall is a comedian, but there are some things that he does not find funny at all. Drugs and alcohol are two of the things. In a February 1992 interview on *The Oprah Winfrey Show*, he revealed that he uses much of his money to buy up "crack" houses so that drug dealers will not have places to sell their drugs.

Choose a cause from the list below and draw a cartoon that expresses your feelings about the issue. (Remember all cartoons do not have to be funny.)

drugs	peace	save the rain forest	ecology
pollution	war	save the dolphins	recycling
nuclear energy	crime	divorce	littering

During the television interview with Oprah Winfrey, Arsenio made the following statements. Read each statement; then respond to each question.

1. "People should learn to appreciate things." Name five things that you appreciate.

2. "I am fascinated to be able to have enough money for myself as well as to help others." What fascinates you?

3. "I like to give gifts." Name three gifts that you would like to get. Name three gifts that you would like to give.

4. "I should take more time for recreation activities." List five places in your city where Arsenio Hall could go for recreation.

5. "I like to spread my wealth helping others." If you suddenly won a sweepstakes and became wealthy, how would you spend your money? To whom or what causes would you spread your wealth?

GA1442

Personal Data

Name: Marva Delores Collins
Birth Year: 1936
Birthplace: Monroeville, Alabama
Field: Education
Occupations: Teacher and school director
Awards and Achievements: Watson Washburn Award for Excellence in Education; Educator of the Year Award; Who's Who in Prestigious America; Who's Who in Black America; Honorary Doctorate degrees from Howard University, Amherst and Dartmouth Colleges

Biographical Information

Marva Collins was born in Monroeville, Alabama, a small rural town located seventy miles north of Mobile. Her father was a well-to-do undertaker who operated his own funeral service. He was also a cattle buyer and merchant. When Marva was old enough, she attended Bethlehem Academy, an old-fashioned elementary school where the teachers were strict and there was no foolishness. Marva became a voracious reader. Because she was black, Marva could not check out books at the local public library, so she had to be content with reading labels on cans, the Farmer's Almanac, the Bible and books that her father bought for her.

In 1953 Marva graduated from high school and went to Clark College in Atlanta. There she earned a degree in secretarial sciences. Afterwards, she taught typing, shorthand and bookkeeping in the Monroe County Alabama school system. In 1969 she decided to move to Chicago. There she worked as a medical secretary at the local hospital. After two years, Marva decided that this type of job was not for her. She wanted to become a teacher again. For fifteen years she taught in Chicago's inner city schools. Many of her students were too poor to buy shoes. So she would skip recess and have her students perform a play or an operetta instead. Because Marva taught in a different way and because her students were achieving so much more than other students, other teachers became jealous of her. Marva became upset. She looked for a place where she could teach her students without interference from anyone.

In 1975 she set out to establish her own school. She used her $5000 retirement money and began a school in her home. At first her class consisted of her daughter and two of her neighbors' children. Later the school was moved to a larger location and enrolled 28 children. With her husband's help, Marva raised money for school supplies and salvaged textbooks from school yard trash cans. Marva developed an unusual school called the Daniel Hale Williams Westside Preparatory School. Many of her students had been told that they would never learn anything. Yet at Marva's school these same students were reading Shakespeare and other high level works of literature. The school day began at 9:00 a.m. and ended at 2:30 p.m. There was no recess, no recreation period, no physical education and only twenty minutes for lunch. Because of her students' achievements and her "no-nonsense" approach to teaching, Marva Collins became famous. She appeared on many television programs such as *60 Minutes*, *The Morton Dean Show*, and *This Is Your Life*. In addition, Marva wrote a book called *The Marva Collins' Way*. It told of her methods of getting students to learn.

31

GA1442

Changes

In order to run a successful school, Marva Collins made changes in what she taught (the curriculum) and how she taught (teaching method).

What changes would you like to see in the following areas of your school? Write them below.

In your classroom _____

_____

_____

In your library _____

_____

_____

In the school cafeteria _____

_____

_____

Design a new and different kind of classroom. Make a sketch of this new classroom in the space below.

Design a student desk that everyone will want to sit in. Make a sketch of the desk in the space below.

Read Any Good Books Lately?

When Marva was growing up she loved to read. But because she was black she was unable to check out books from the local public library.

Times have changed and people of all ages and backgrounds can check out and read books of their choice. Can you recommend some good books for students your age?

1. Book Title_____

    Summary of Book (what the book is about)_____

    _____

2. Book Title_____

    Summary of Book _____

    _____

3. Book Title_____

    Summary of Book _____

    _____

4. Book Title_____

    Summary of Book _____

    _____

Pick one of the above books as your favorite. _____

Tell why it is your favorite.

GA1442

I'm Special

Marva Collins feels that everyone of her students is a unique person. She teaches her students that there is something about each one of them that makes them special.

Think about the things that make you special; complete the inventory below.

Name: _____   Favorite Food: _____

Age: _____   Favorite TV Program: _____

Birth Date: _____   Favorite Ice-Cream Flavor: _____

Weight: _____   Favorite Pizza Topping: _____

Height: _____   Favorite Song: _____

Eye Color: _____   Favorite Color: _____

Favorite Person: _____   Hobbies: _____

Make an "I'm Special" box. Cut out pictures from magazines that show things that you like. Paste these pictures on the inside and outside of a shoe box. Share and compare your box with a friend. How are the two of you alike? How are the two of you different? Take your box home and share it with your parents.

GA1442

Creativity 4

Name Change

In 1975 Marva Collins quit teaching in the Chicago city school system, checked out $5000 of her own retirement money and started a school of her own. She named it the Daniel Hale Williams Westside Preparatory School in honor of the great African American surgeon Dr. Daniel Hale Williams. Research and write a paragraph of information about Dr. Daniel Hale Williams.

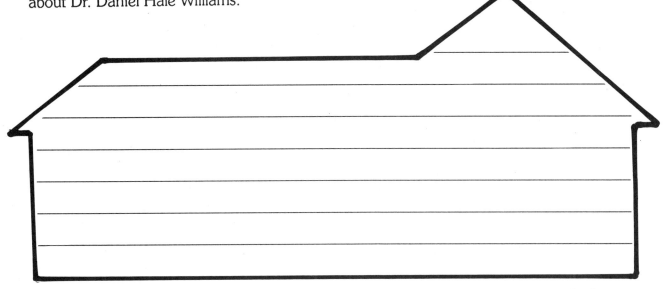

What is the name of your school? Is it named for a famous person? If so, try to find some information about the famous person. Ask your teacher, parents, principal and librarian to help you. If you could rename your school for a famous person, who would that person be? Write a paragraph of information to convince your board of education that your school name should be changed to honor your famous person.

GA1442

Big Changes

For starting a new type of school and a new way to teach, Marva Collins appeared on many television programs. The money that she received from the Hallmark Hall of Fame CBS television special, *The Marva Collins' Story,* was used to move her school to a better location.

With a money grant from Prince, the famous rock star and singer, Marva Collins' started a teacher training program to teach her methods to other teachers. Marva Collins' teaching program includes twenty minutes for lunch, no recess and no P.E. or gym. Five-year-old students read Aesops Fables instead of "Dick and Jane" books. Older students read such literary works as *Macbeth, Paradise Lost* and the *Painted Bird.*

What do you think about Marva Collins' teaching methods? Suppose that you have recently been appointed curriculum director for your school district. List five new subjects that you would add to the curriculum.

Write a paragraph of information telling why you think students should or should not have P.E. or gym.

1. _____

    _____

2. _____

    _____

3. _____

    _____

4. _____

    _____

5. _____

    _____

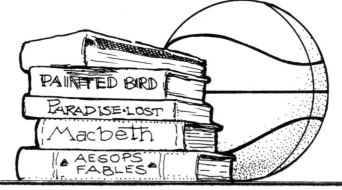

Personal Data

Name: George Carruthers
Birth Year: 1940
Birthplace: Chicago, Illinois
Field: Science
Occupation: Astrophysicist
Awards and Achievements: NASA Special Achievement Award

Biographical Information

When George Carruthers was a young boy, he loved to look at the stars. On a clear night he could be found in his bedroom window gazing into the night sky. As he grew, so did his fascination for astronomy. At times, he would spend hour after hour reading about the stars and planets. When he was ten years old, he built his first telescope and his formal study of astronomy began. As he grew older he began to think about turning his interest in astronomy into a career.

George became interested in space and space travel. But he soon grew discouraged because those who listened to him tell of his dream to travel in space called his ideas silly. His father didn't think that his ideas were silly. He supported George and encouraged him to follow his interest. He told George that he could be anything that he wished if he were willing to work hard enough. But when George was twelve years old a tragic thing happened, his father died and there was no one to support him and his ideas. But that didn't stop George. By this time he had grown determined that he would grow up to be a space scientist. He completed high school and made plans to attend college. When George told his mother, she was worried. She wondered where she would get the money to send him to college.

Since the death of his father, money had been tight. But George refused to abandon his hopes of going to college and studying astronomy. He looked for a way to fulfill his dream, and he found a way. His grades were good so he was able to get a scholarship and work part-time to help with his college costs. George chose to go into engineering instead of astronomy because he felt that he could contribute more to the field of space science by developing new ideas and techniques. George received his college degree and continued his education. First he earned his master's degree and then a Ph.D. degree in Aeronautical Engineering. In 1972 he used his engineering skills and his knowledge of astronomy to help him develop the camera that was used in the Apollo Moon Mission. Because of this achievement, he was awarded NASA's Special Achievement Award. George's dream of becoming involved in the space program has come true. Today he works hard at his job as senior astrophysicist for the nation's largest space agency, NASA.

GA1442

Creativity 1

Career Collage

George Carruthers turned his interest in astronomy into a career in space science. Use this page to make a career collage. Look through magazines and cut out pictures and words that are related to what you want to be in life.

Glue the pictures and words on this sheet. Use a magic marker to add your own personal touch. Show your collage to a friend. Can he/she tell from the pictures and words what you want to be in life? Display your collage in the classroom for others to see.

GA1442

Blazing a Path to the Stars

To begin, select a word from either of the start positions. Find information about the word in a dictionary or encyclopedia. On the back of this page write the word and its definition. Use a crayon or marker to color each hexagonal word space as you complete each word. Continue choosing and coloring until you blaze a path of your choice to the stars at the finish.

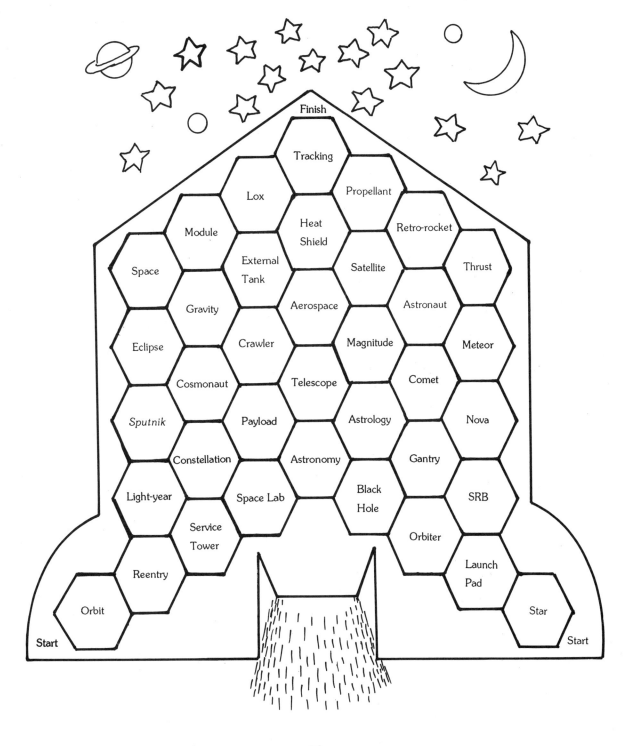

Creativity 3

Find and Follow Your Dream

"Climb every mountain, ford every stream,
Follow every rainbow
'til you find your dream."
These words were taken from *The Sound of Music*. What do you think these words mean?
Write your meaning in the space below.

_____

_____

_____

_____

_____

_____

_____

In the clouds below write some words of your own encouraging people to find and follow their dreams.

Lost in Space

Once while traveling in space, your ship made a crash landing on planet Octor in a place called Octorville. Much of the equipment aboard your craft was damaged or lost. Luckily your instamatic camera was still intact. You began to take pictures. In the boxes below, show the pictures that you took.

The average Octovillian looked like this.

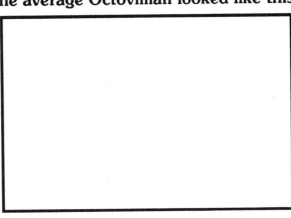

This is what their home looked like.

Here is a picture of their car.

This is a picture of their school.

The grocery store looked like this.

GA1442

Complete these sentences on this page to continue telling about your trip in space.

1. Their food was as hard as a _____ and it tasted like _____.

2. They slept standing up wrapped in a _____.

3. Their hair was _____, and it felt like _____.

4. Their clothes were _____. They had plenty _____, but they had

   no _____.

5. They grew apples as large as a _____. They were so large that you

   could _____.

6. They had _____ ears, and they wore a hat made of _____.

7. Instead of using spoons and forks for eating, they used _____ and

   _____.

8. Their shoes were large. The babies wore size _____, and the grown-ups

   wore size _____.

9. Their hands had only _____ fingers and a thumb that was _____.

10. Everywhere they went they carried a large _____ filled with _____.

GA1442

Memory Wall

Tragedy struck the U.S. space program on January 27, 1967, when three Apollo astronauts were killed on the launch pad at the John F. Kennedy Space Center in Florida. On January 28, 1986, tragedy struck again.

This time the space shuttle *Challenger* exploded and seven crew members lost their lives. Among the crew members were Ronald McNair, an African American astronaut, and Christa McAuliffe, a teacher.

In memory of Ronald McNair, Christa McAuliffe and the other five astronauts who lost their lives in the space program, complete the activities on the memory wall below.

	1. Draw and color a sunset.	
2. How are you like a star?	3. Research and write three informative sentences about Guion Bluford.	4. What color is January? Why?
5. What would you name your spaceship?	6. Create a new space shuttle.	7. Write a haiku about space.
8. Draw and color a rainbow.	9. Make five words from the word *Challenger*.	10. Would you like to travel in outer space? Where would you visit?

GA1442

Personal Data

Name: Wynton Marsalis
Birth Year: 1961
Birthplace: New Orleans, Louisiana
Fields: Arts and entertainment
Occupations: Jazz and classical musician and trumpet player
Awards and Achievements: Considered to be one of the world's greatest trumpet players, only musician to win a Grammy award for jazz and a Grammy award for classical music the same year

Biographical Information

When you think of famous African American musicians, chances are that you think of such rock stars as Michael Jackson, Stevie Wonder or M.C. Hammer. There is an African American musician who is just as famous as they are. He is famous in two fields of different kinds of music. He is a famous jazz and classical musician. Wynton Marsalis is his name. He is a most gifted and learned musician. In fact, in 1984 he accomplished what no other musician had ever accomplished before. He won Grammy awards for both jazz and classical music and became known the world over as the greatest trumpet player of all times.

Wynton's early interest in music was influenced by his parents. You could say that it was in his family's blood. He comes from a musically talented family. His father composes music, plays the piano and teaches music. His mother sings, and his oldest brother plays the saxophone. When Wynton was six years old, he received his first musical instrument. It was a trumpet that was given to him by Al Hirt, a famous jazz musician. When Wynton was twelve years old, he became serious about his music. He began taking trumpet lessons. During his teen years when most teenagers are infatuated by rock and roll music, Wynton spent his time buying, playing and practicing jazz and classical music.

Throughout his teen years, he refined his musical abilities by playing in marching and jazz bands. In the years that followed, in his hometown of New Orleans, he took advantage of every opportunity. He joined the New Orleans Civic Orchestra and listened to such great jazz artists as Louis Armstrong, Miles Davis and John Coltrane. Growing up in New Orleans also gave him a chance to attend concerts and performances of other great jazz musicians. In the 1980's Wynton began recording music of his own. It is a great accomplishment to be very good at one style of music, but to be very good at two different styles of music is an even greater accomplishment. Wynton Marsalis' mastery of both jazz and classical music places him in a category all by himself.

44

GA1442

The Day the Music Died

Think for a moment—what would the world be like if there were no music? Make a list of all of the many different and unusual changes that would take place if there were no music. Be original; try to think up changes that no one else will think of.

Example:
1. There would be no national anthems.
2. People would dance to the "all talk" radio stations.

_____

_____

_____

_____

_____

_____

_____

_____

_____

_____

_____

_____

_____

_____

_____

Use the back of this page to write a brief story entitled "The Day the Music Died." Make your story interesting, creative and fun to read.

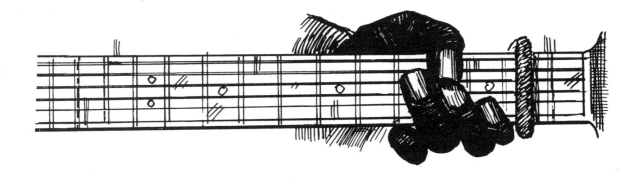

GA1442

Musical Instruments

Do you play a musical instrument? Do you know someone who does? Wynton Marsalis plays the trumpet. He has been hailed as the world's greatest trumpet player. The trumpet belongs to a group of musical instruments called brass instruments. Brass instruments have long tubes with a mouthpiece at one end and a flared opening called a bell at the other end. Some brass instruments have valves. Other instruments in the brass group include the cornet, bugle, trombone, and tuba. Besides this group of instruments, there are five other groups–stringed instruments, woodwind instruments, keyboard instruments, and percussion instruments. How much do you know about these groups of instruments? Complete the chart to learn more.

Musical Instruments Chart

Major Instrument Group	How Music Is Produced	Examples of Instruments in This Group
Example: Brass	Music is produced by blowing air through tubes with a mouthpiece at one end and a bell at the other.	trumpet, cornet, bugle, trombone and tuba
Stringed Instruments		
Woodwind Instruments		
Keyboard Instruments		
Percussion Instruments		

GA1442

Jazz Hall of Fame

You are part of a committee to select five famous jazz musicians to be inducted into the Jazz Hall of Fame. You have to make your selections from the list of fifteen nominees below. Which five musicians will you select for this great honor? For each musician that you select, you must write three brief statements about the life of that person to tell why you are nominating him/her. Do research to help you with this part. Here is the list of nominees. Dizzy Gillespie, Louis Armstrong, Bessie Smith, Ella Fitzgerald, Lionel Hampton, John Coltrane, Miles Davis, Billie Holiday, Count Basie, Duke Ellington, Herbie Hancock, Charlie Parker, Fats Waller, Scott Joplin, Thelonious Monk.

Write the names of your five choices in the Jazz Hall of Fame. Write your three statements beneath each name.

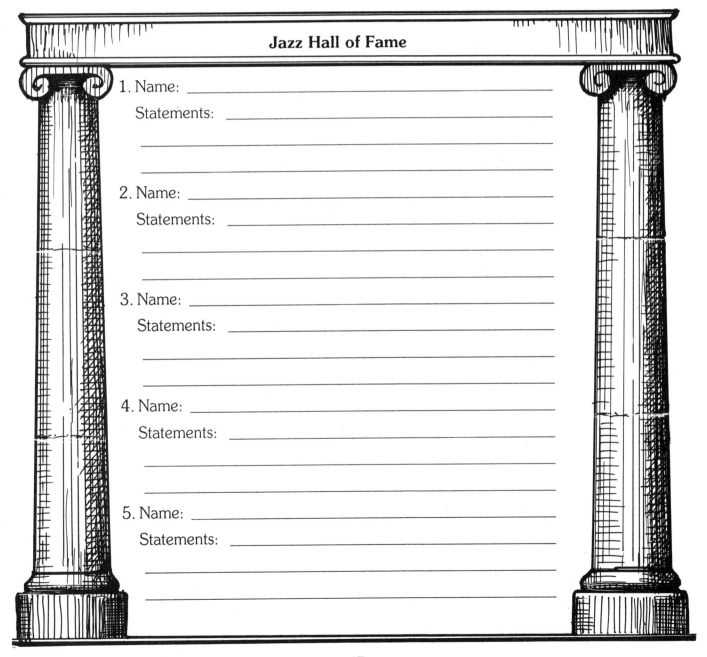

Jazz Hall of Fame

1. Name: _____
   Statements: _____
   _____
   _____

2. Name: _____
   Statements: _____
   _____
   _____

3. Name: _____
   Statements: _____
   _____
   _____

4. Name: _____
   Statements: _____
   _____
   _____

5. Name: _____
   Statements: _____
   _____
   _____

GA1442

Search and Find

Music comes in a variety of forms and kinds. Fourteen different kinds are hidden in the puzzle below. Can you find all of them?

When you have found them all, underline the two types of music that Wynton Marsalis plays and put a check beside the kind of music that you like. Use the words below to help you.

```
K L K X I Z Y R Z D D Y N P Y
X H X Y U R K T Z L J E V U I
Q W W Z T E L L A B J I V O M
M Z Y N Z L Y G O P B Q P F C
P L U Q E A W Y Y F P J U M R
L O G J H C J C L K Z Z M W Y
C O P V M I S V B H L K A G D
U H Y U G S X A C F E T N U E
R U G H L S L N E O T D K X M
K Y P H E A L H H E V Q M C O
C T Y G M L R K R E B M A H C
Y I R G I C E E X L U I H J S
G R L O T R P C M S M K O C R
J Q X R G O R A T O R I O E H
F Z U G A P C U B R A V J Y C
P T R R R E Z R Z I O Z M L V
Y S F U Z R O C K S H N V L S
O J T Z V A Q Q B P N M I J A
I A F D C W E P G J D E I C O
```

Can you find these words?

electronic	classical	oratorio
operetta	ragtime	popular
country	chamber	rock
ballet	opera	folk
jazz	hymn	

GA1442

Music Poster

Some people believe that more people would appreciate the classical and jazz styles of music if they would take time to listen to it. Design a poster that would encourage people to listen to jazz or classical music. Make a miniaturized version of your poster in the space below.

GA1442

Personal Data

Name: Florence Griffith Joyner
Birth Year: 1959
Birthplace: Los Angeles, California
Field: Sports
Occupation: Track and field star
Awards and Achievements: French Sportswoman of the Year (1988), Athlete of the Year by Soviet Union News Agency Tass (1988), United States Olympic Committee Award, Golden Camera Award in Berlin, Harvard Foundation Award, Jesse Owens Award (1988), Sullivan Award, silver medal at 1984 Summer Olympics, gold medal in 1988 Summer Olympics

Biographical Information

Florence Griffith Joyner was the seventh child of eleven children of Robert Griffith, an electronics technician, and Florence Griffith a seamstress. Her parents divorced when she was four years old. Her mother moved the children to a housing project in Los Angeles, California. To avoid confusion with her mother's name, Florence was called Dee Dee. When Dee Dee was seven years old, she began running track. During her elementary and junior high school years, Dee Dee won many awards and a medal for her track activities. When she was fourteen years old, she won the Jesse Owens National Youth Games Award and was congratulated personally by the famous track and field star himself. In 1978 Florence Griffith (Dee Dee) Joyner graduated from high school and enrolled at California State University at Northridge. She had intended to study business, but her money ran out and she had to drop out of college. But Dee Dee was not the kind of person to give up. She got a job as a bank teller, saved her money and returned to college at U.C.L.A., where she trained under Coach Bob Kersee. With training and encouragement from her family and friends, Dee Dee set many new records in track and field. She trained for the Olympics and won a silver medal in 1984. She was disappointed because she did not win the gold medal and dropped out of training for a while. But in 1987 she decided to train again for the 1988 Olympics. She began a rigorous training program. In the Olympic trials she set new records and became the most talked about young athlete in the world.

Her picture appeared on the covers of such famous magazines as *Newsweek, Sports Illustrated, Life, Ebony, Jet* and *Ms.* She was also recognized by German, Japanese, and French magazines. At the summer Olympics of 1988 in Seoul, South Korea, she won four medals (three golds and one silver) and set a world record in both the 100 and 200-meter events. Immediately following the Olympic Games, Florence Griffith Joyner received many offers to advertise products, star in movies and TV commercials, give speeches and appear on major television shows. Florence Griffith Joyner became known as "Flo Jo," a name that reminded everyone of her grace and speed. In the winter of 1989 Flo Jo announced that she was retiring from track to follow her interests in writing, acting, designing and modeling. Flo Jo had made her mark on history, and now she wanted to move on to achieve in other areas of her life.

Healthy Advice

When Florence Griffith Joyner won the Jesse Owens National Youth Games Award, she was congratulated personally by the famous track and field star. As a child, Jesse Owens was sickly. A coach once told him to run every day to strengthen his body and keep it healthy. Jesse Owens followed his advice and became a world famous track star. He represented the United States in the 1936 Olympics. He broke many track records and won four Olympic gold medals.

List several activities that you can do to keep your body healthy and strong. Draw a picture of yourself doing one of the activities.

1. Stay away from alcohol and drugs.   4. _____

2. _____   5. _____

3. _____   6. _____

A proverb is a short sentence that tells a truth or gives some bit of useful information. "Early to bed and early to rise, makes a person healthy, wealthy and wise" is such a proverb.

Write a "healthy" proverb of your own and explain what it means.

_____

_____

_____

_____

_____

_____

Nicknames

Because of her speed and smoothness in running, Florence Griffith Joyner was given the nickname "Flo Jo." Several other famous athletes have been given nicknames. Their real names are listed below.

Can you give the nickname and the sport each played? Some of the blanks have been filled in for you.

Name	Nickname/Other Name	Sport
1. O.J. Simpson	Orange Juice	football
2. Leroy Paige	_____	_____
3. Julius Ervin	_____	_____
4. Ervin Johnson	Magic Johnson	_____
5. Wilt Chamberlain	_____	_____
6. Joe Louis	_____	boxing
7. Cassius Clay	_____	_____
8. William Perry	The Refrigerator	_____
9. Henry Aaron	_____	_____
10. Ray Robinson	_____	boxing

Survey your class to find out how many of your classmates have nicknames. Write their real names first and their nicknames last.

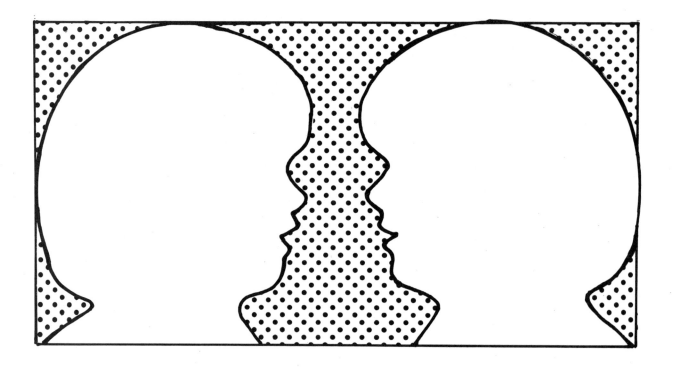

GA1442

Creativity 3

A Circle of Friends

When it comes to outstanding performance in track and field, Florence Griffith Joyner is not alone. Listed below are the names of five famous African Americans whose names appear in the Track and Field Hall of Fame in Indianapolis, Indiana. Unscramble the letters to reveal each name. Write the name in the numbered space. Use the names in the name bank to help you. Select one of the names and write an information paragraph about that person. On the back of the sheet draw a "circle of friends" for yourself. See if others can unscramble the names.

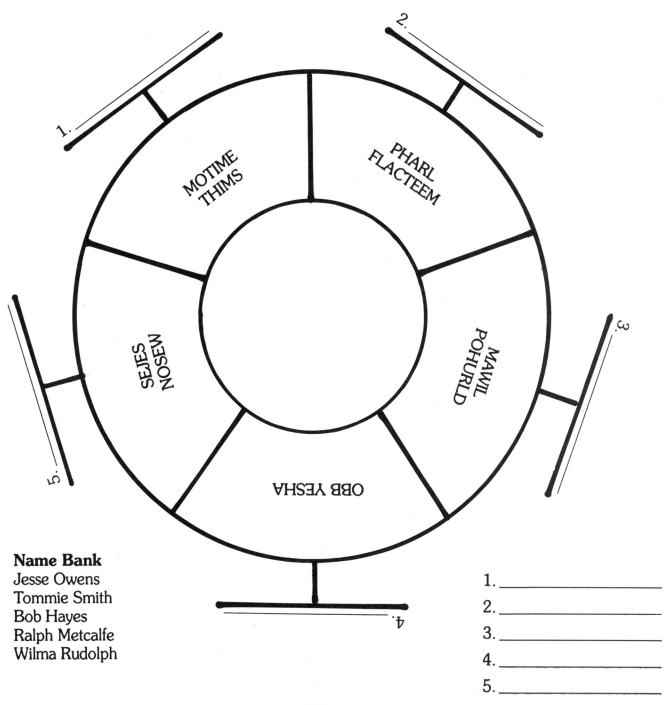

Name Bank
Jesse Owens
Tommie Smith
Bob Hayes
Ralph Metcalfe
Wilma Rudolph

1. _____
2. _____
3. _____
4. _____
5. _____

Creativity 4

★★★★★★★★★ And Three to Go ★★★★★★★★★

Three famous track and field stars overcame physical disabilities to reach their goals. They were Wilma Rudolph, Jesse Owens and Jackie Joyner-Kersee. They all had one thing in common–they wanted to succeed and were willing to work hard to achieve their goals.

You have been asked to speak to a gathering of young handicapped persons to encourage them to participate in physical activities. Research information about the three famous track and field stars and use the information in your speech. Write what you will say in the space below.

GA1442

Just for the Record

Florence Griffith Joyner is a winner. In the 1988 Olympics Games she set a world record in both the 100 meter and 200-meter events. It's time to find out about the record setters in your class. Who is the best speller? The best in math? Search among your classmates to find the record setters in each area below.

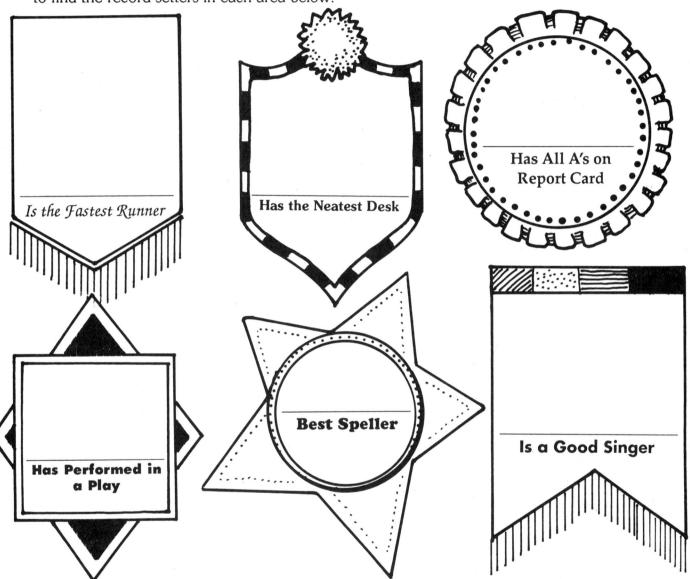

Is the Fastest Runner

Has the Neatest Desk

Has All A's on
Report Card

**Has Performed in
a Play**

Best Speller

Is a Good Singer

Use the *Guinness Book of World Records* to record ten different record holders and the areas in which they hold records.

1. _____
2. _____
3. _____
4. _____
5. _____

6. _____
7. _____
8. _____
9. _____
10. _____

Personal Data

Name: Oprah Winfrey
Birth Year: 1954
Birthplace: Kosciusko, Mississippi
Field: Entertainment
Occupations: Daytime television talk show host, actor and producer
Awards and Achievements: 1987 Emmy award for best talk show hostess, 1986 Woman Achievement Award, Golden Globe Nomination, Chicago Academy for the Arts Award, 1991 Steuben Crystal Award

Biographical Information

The Oprah Winfrey story is a true story of "rags to riches." Oprah was born on a farm in the state of Mississippi to Vernita and Vernon Winfrey. Her parents soon separated. Her father moved to Nashville, Tennessee, and her mother moved to Milwaukee, Wisconsin. Oprah was left with her grandmother on the farm. As a little girl, Oprah dreamed of becoming an actress. When she became lonely on the farm, she would entertain herself by pretending that the cows and chickens were her audience and that she was an actress.

When Oprah was six years old, she left the farm and went to live in Milwaukee with her mother. Oprah was still lonely. Now she didn't even have the farm animals for company. Without her farm animals and money to buy a dog, she kept a jar of cockroaches as pets. By this time, Oprah was being reared partly by her father in Nashville and partly by her mother in Wisconsin. Once while she was visiting her father, she gave a speech at a church gathering. The church people were astonished by the way she spoke. Soon, other churches began asking her to speak for them. When she was twelve years old she had earned over five hundred dollars as a speaker. Oprah liked to speak, but she liked it even better when she was paid for her speeches.

When Oprah became a teenager, she was still a lonely child; she felt unloved and unwanted. In order to draw attention to herself, she began to get into trouble. Once she faked a robbery by storming her house and breaking out the windows. When her mother felt that she could no longer handle her, she sent her to live with her father in Nashville, Tennessee. Even though Oprah did not think so, this was one of the best things that would happen to her. Her father was very strict with her. He showed her love and attention, but he also provided her with the guidance that she needed to change her life. Under his guidance, Oprah was required to learn at least five new vocabulary words each day. She also had to read one book every week. Oprah began to excel in her schoolwork, too.

At the age of sixteen she won a speaking contest and received a scholarship to a major university in Tennessee. While attending college she became a reporter for a local television station. After graduating from college she became co-anchor for the evening news at a television station in Baltimore. Her climb to success had begun. In January 1984, Oprah moved to Chicago and became anchor of a morning television show. She did so well that she was given her own show, *The Oprah Winfrey Show.* The next year, her dream of becoming an actor came true. She starred in a movie called *The Color Purple.* She received many awards and honors for her role in this movie.

Oprah Winfrey is now a famous person. She is an actress. She has bought her own film and television studio, and she has her own afternoon talk show with millions of viewers. In 1987 *The Oprah Winfrey Show* won an Emmy award for television's best talk show, and Oprah won an Emmy for best talk-show host. When you think of how successful Oprah has become, it is hard to believe that she was once a lonely, poor farm girl from a small town in Mississippi.

Oprah's Alphabet

In order to increase her vocabulary, Oprah's father required her to learn at least five new words each day. Give your vocabulary a boost. Use a dictionary to find a new word for each letter in Oprah's name. Write the meaning of the word and use it correctly in a sentence.

Alphabet	New Word	Meaning	Sentence
O			
P			
R			
A			
H			
W			
I			
N			
F			
R			
E			
Y			

GA1442

Bouncing Back

When Oprah was young her parents divorced and Oprah was shifted from one parent to the other. When she became a teenager, she felt ignored, lonely and rejected. In order to call attention to herself, she began to get into trouble. Almost everyone has felt rejected at one time or another. It is not the rejection itself that causes problems. It is how the person reacts to the rejection.

Do you see yourself in these examples?
1. You can learn easily and remember more than anyone in your class, but you didn't get a part in the spring play.
2. When students were choosing team members for the softball game, no one chose you.
3. You have raised your hand a million times, but the teacher always calls on someone else to recite.
4. You thought you were going to get inducted into the Honor Society, but when all of the names were called, yours wasn't.

Rejection is a hurting experience. But the thing to remember about rejection is that it is not the end of the world. You can develop your own plan or strategy for coping with rejection. Then when it comes along you will be ready. If you do not have a plan, chances are that you will react in a negative way and become deeply hurt by it.

When you feel rejected, think of yourself as a rubber ball hitting a brick wall–learn to bounce back. Let your mind return to pleasant thoughts before the rejection came along. Think of rejection as an ice-cream cone on a hot summer day. In your mind, let the rejection melt away and clean up the mess. Another way is to think of rejection as a helium-filled balloon. Deal with it; then release the rejection and watch it float away.

Talk with your school guidance counselor about other ways of dealing with rejection. Now go back to the examples and develop a plan of what you would do in each situation. Write your plan for examples 1, 2 and 3 below.

1. _____

2. _____

3. _____

Create and illustrate three bumper stickers about rejection.

Guest of Honor

Having to schedule a guest or guests for each day of every week could be a problem. But Oprah Winfrey has always been able to have fresh new guests with fresh new topics and ideas every day of the week. However, Oprah is looking for a new guest and new topics for the second week in February. Since February is Black History Month, she has decided to invite famous African Americans for this week. Choose the names of five African Americans from the African American Hall of Fame to appear on the talk show.

Research and write beside each chosen famous African American's name the topic on which the person is qualified to speak. Write a day of the week on which the person will speak beside each selected name. You will be the invited guest for Wednesday of the second week. What will be your topic? Write a two-minute speech on your topic. Use the back of this sheet if you have to.

African American Hall of Fame

Check Here to Choose	Name	Topic	Day of Week to Speak
	Guion Bluford		
	Marva Collins		
	Colin Powell		
	Mae Jemison		
	Douglas Wilder		
	Cicely Tyson		
	Whitney Houston		
	James Baldwin		
	Michael Jordan		
√	(your name)		Wednesday

Book It!

When Oprah Winfrey was growing up, she liked to curl up in a chair and read a good book. When she felt lonely she would read. She could solve mysteries with the Hardy Boys or Nancy Drew, explore the prairie with the Ingalls family or float on a raft with Huckleberry Finn. Her reading took her to the bottom of the sea with Moby Dick or far into space on a Star Trek mission.

List the title of five good books on the book covers below. On the lines beneath tell where each book will take the reader.

This book will take you to _____ _____
_____ _____ _____
_____ _____ _____

Award Presentation

Oprah Winfrey won an Emmy award for best talk show host. Since then she has won numerous awards, recognitions and honors. In 1991 she was awarded the Steuben Crystal Award in recognition for the many humanitarian deeds that she has done. These include donating large sums of money to black colleges and universities and contributing to scholarships, charities and other worthwhile endeavors. Imagine that Oprah Winfrey has donated $1.5 million dollars for a new recreation center in your hometown. The center is complete and Oprah has been invited back to a banquet to receive the Good Giver Award at a banquet. It is your job to present the award. Follow the outline below to help you plan your presentation speech.

1. Greet the audience and welcome them to the occasion. (Write what you will say here.)
2. Give the reason for the award and give the name of the group that is giving the award.
3. Briefly tell why the person deserves the award.
4. Call the person up to receive the award. "Will Mr./Mrs./Ms. _____ please come forward?"
5. While the person is coming forward, hold the award up for all to see.
6. When the person arrives (on stage), call his/her name.
7. Hand the award to the person.
8. Wait for the acceptance speech. When it has ended you may sit.

Choose a class partner and pretend that the person is Oprah Winfrey. Practice your presentation. Exchange places and let your partner present you with an award. Choose a presentation situation below and practice again.

1. A trophy to an outstanding athlete of your school
2. A trophy to the principal who is retiring
3. A bouquet of flowers to a retiring teacher
4. A trophy to a winning volleyball team
5. A plaque for a first place performance of the school band

Personal Data

Name: Stevie Wonder
Birth Year: 1950
Birthplace: Saginaw, Michigan
Fields: Arts and entertainment
Occupation: Musician, composer, songwriter, and singer
Awards and Achievements: Graduated from high school with honors, recorded his first gold record at the age of twelve, won fifteen Grammy awards from 1973-1985, Distinguished Service Award for Outstanding Achievement in the World of Entertainment, Show Business Inspiration Award

Biographical Information

In 1950 a baby boy was born to Mrs. Lula Mae Hardaway of Saginaw, Michigan. It was not long before she realized that her son was blind. She was disappointed at first, but she soon realized that her son was a very talented child. She became determined that her little "Stevie" would be given every opportunity to become successful in life. When he was old enough, she enrolled him in the Michigan School for the Blind, where he learned Braille. When Stevie showed an interest in music, his mother arranged for him to take music lessons.

First, Stevie began to master the piano; then he began to play the harmonica. One day his mother took him to a picnic and someone set him behind a set of drums. Before long, Stevie had learned to master the drums too. Stevie made so much progress so fast that he became known as "Stevie Wonder."

In 1962 when he was only twelve years old he recorded his first hit. It was called "Fingertips." It was followed by one smash hit after another. Not long afterwards, Stevie Wonder was no longer the little blind boy from a Detroit housing project. Stevie Wonder was a musical genius known the world over. His talents were not limited to the field of music. Stevie Wonder also appeared in two motion pictures and several major television shows.

Those who know Stevie Wonder say that his success has not spoiled him. They say that he still remains a happy guy who cares about himself as well as others. Stevie Wonder gives much of the credit for his success to his mother. Early in his life, she taught him that "a handicap isn't a handicap unless you make it one." His mother has always been a great encouragement to him. She even wrote the words for one of his best-selling songs. In the 1990's Stevie Wonder has become one of the greatest entertainers in the history of popular music. His success continues to grow, and he continues to be an inspiration for others, especially those who are handicapped as he is.

Gifts

Stevie Wonder believes that his musical abilities are a gift from God that he uses to make people happy. What special abilities or talents do you have? Can you play soccer really well? Do you play the piano? Write a special gift or talent that you have in each gift package below.

Imagine that you are baby-sitting a three-year-old toddler. The child begins to cry. He is not sick or hurt. You want to entertain him so that he will stop crying. You look around you and find the following objects: a comb, bucket, pieces of paper, a string, a ball, a flashlight, a spoon, an empty cereal box and an old wind-up clock. Tell how you would use each object or combination of objects to entertain the child and save your job.

Make a list of all the things that you could use these items for. Be creative!

1. _____
2. _____
3. _____
4. _____
5. _____
6. _____
7. _____
8. _____

9. _____
10. _____
11. _____
12. _____
13. _____
14. _____
15. _____
16. _____

GA1442

Smiling Faces

Stevie Wonder uses his music to make people happy. Happiness means different things to different people. In the smiley faces below list fifteen different things that make you happy.

In the five sad faces write things that make you sad.

GA1442

Code 1

Use these musical notes and symbols to decode these messages about Stevie Wonder.

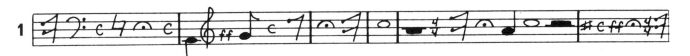

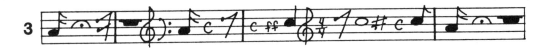

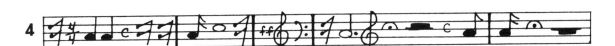

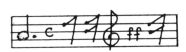

Use the code to write your own message about Stevie Wonder on the back of this sheet. Ask a classmate to solve your coded message.

GA1442

Handicapped

The word *handicapped* means "to have a disability that interferes with a person's ability to lead a normal life." Stevie Wonder has a handicap; he is blind. When his mother learned that her son was blind, she was disappointed at first. Afterwards she decided that she would help her child to become all that he could be. She told him, "A handicap is not a handicap unless you make it one."

What do you think she meant by that statement? Many handicapped persons are able to overcome their handicaps to make remarkable contributions and achievements. Such is the life of Stevie Wonder. Despite his handicap, he has excelled to become one of the most famous musicians in the world. Complete the following activities to get a "feel" for being blind.

1. Let a classmate blindfold you and give you an unfamiliar object. Describe its every detail; then try to identify it.
2. Using steps and right turns or left turns, make a map from your classroom to the school library. Blindfold a friend. Call out the directions and see if your friend can follow them. How accurate is your map? Was your friend able to find the library? Switch so that you are blindfolded. Follow a map that your friend makes from your classroom to the cafeteria.
3. Most blind persons have developed a keen sense of hearing and touch. Go outside, sit down and close your eyes. What can you learn about your surroundings by listening and touching?
4. Blindfold yourself and let your friend find a picture of an object in a catalog or magazine. The friend can give only five clues. Afterwards you may ask only five questions about the object. Can you tell what the object is from the clues and questions? Exchange places and repeat with your friend.

Complete these activities to learn more about the blind.
1. Research the life of Helen Keller.
2. Write to the National Blindness Information Center (one per class) for information on blindness and careers and jobs in helping the blind.
   1800 Johnson Street
   Baltimore, MD 21230
3. Research eye banks and guide dogs.
4. Research the Braille method of reading.
5. Using glue, cardboard and small pebbles, construct a Braille system. Blindfold a friend. Can your friend spell out his/her name in Braille? Can you spell out your name while blindfolded?

Name Dropper

For more than 200 years African Americans have played and enjoyed music. First, during slavery there were work songs and spirituals. Afterwards came ragtime, blues and then jazz. In the 1940's rhythm and blues was the favorite kind of music. It was rock 'n' roll in the 1950's, soul music in the 1960's, and funk and disco in the 1970's. The 1980's and 1990's saw a different form of music; it was called rap. Rap is poetry or verse chanted to music with a heavy beat. In the early 1990's rap took the country by storm. One of the widely known performers of rap is M.C. Hammer. "Hammer," as he is called, has not only influenced the music world but movies, radio and television advertisements have also been influenced by his style of music. Twenty-five African American musicians are listed below. Their first names have been dropped. Can you pick the correct name from the name bank and write it in the blank space beside each name?

Name Bank

Chuck	Michael	Stevie	Anita
Whitney	Aretha	Chubby	Count
Natalie	Stephanie	Patti	Bessie
Thelonious	Luther	Miles	Ella
W.C.	Duke	Lionel	Dizzy
M.C.	Scott	Mahalia	Fats
Lionel			

1. _____ Smith
2. _____ Waller
3. _____ Monk
4. _____ Hampton
5. _____ Jackson
6. _____ Handy
7. _____ Joplin
8. _____ Gillespie
9. _____ Fitzgerald
10. _____ Ellington
11. _____ Davis
12. _____ Cole
13. _____ Basie

14. _____ Houston
15. _____ Vandross
16. _____ LaBelle
17. _____ Hammer
18. _____ Jackson
19. _____ Franklin
20. _____ Wonder
21. _____ Richie
22. _____ Mills
23. _____ Berry
24. _____ Checker
25. _____ Baker

Place a star beside two of your favorite African American musicians. Research their lives and use the information to write a rap or poem about each life.

GA1442

Personal Data

Name: Eldrick "Tiger" Woods
Birth Year: 1976
Birthplace: Cypress, California
Awards and Achievements: The youngest player and the first Black to win the U.S. Junior Amateur Golf Championship. Eldrick was featured in a documentary film entitled *Black History, 1991*. The film focused on major events and accomplishments of outstanding African Americans in the year 1991.

Biographical Information

"Here comes the Tiger" is what everyone says when fifteen-year-old Eldrick Woods walks on the golf course. Eldrick earned the nickname "Tiger" because of his quick and accurate moves on the golf course. When he was a small child, he watched his father play golf. When he was a toddler, his father noticed him trying to hit a golf ball into a net. At the age of three, he gained national attention when he competed with Bob Hope in a putting contest on *The Mike Douglas* Show. When he was six years old, he reportedly hit a hole in one and became the youngest person ever to accomplish such a difficult task. After that, Eldrick "Tiger" Woods was swinging golf clubs and winning all kinds of trophies and awards. In 1991 at the age of fifteen, Tiger became the youngest person ever to win the U.S. Junior Amateur Golf Championship. Since then he has become an international golf sensation.

Even though golfing takes him away from home and sometimes away from his studies, Tiger still manages to earn a 3.5 grade average on a 4.0 scale. He plans to complete high school, get a college education and then become a professional golfer. His goal is to be better than Jack Nicklaus, one that Tiger believes is the best ever. Tiger states that he wants to be the Michael Jordan of golf. This means that he wants to bring the kind of excitement and skills to golf that Michael Jordan has brought to basketball. Tiger's parents say that he has learned both responsibility and self-discipline from the game. His parents say that he does his schoolwork and practices golf without ever being pushed or prodded, because he realizes that both are important if he is to reach the goals that he has set for himself.

Tiger's mother and father take turns driving him to golf tournaments and other related activities. Tiger knows that good athletes are paid extremely well, but he says that he is not in it for the money. He says that he plays for the love of the game. His involvement in golf has spurred others to become interested in the game as well. Because of his good grades and great golf skills, Tiger has already been contacted by several colleges and universities, but he figures that he has plenty of time to make that decision. Tiger Woods is breaking one record after another on the golf course and because he is, he is constantly being interviewed by the news media. He says that the interviews can be a problem sometimes, because they take up so much of his time. Tiger wants to be the youngest player ever to win the PGA (Professional Golfers' Association of America) title. Many people think that he has a good chance to do just that. What do you think?

68

Creativity 1

Origination

Do you play golf? Do you know someone who does? Chances are that you do, because golf is one of the most popular outdoor sports in the world. Millions of men, women and children play golf, and millions more watch golf games either as spectators or at home on television. Golf is thought to have originated as a Roman or Dutch game. It is said that golf was first played in the United States as early as the 1700's. How about your favorite sport? When and where did it originate? Research and write about the origin of your favorite sport. How well do you know your sport? Can you explain how your sport is played to someone who has never seen the game before? Try to in the space below.

_____

_____

_____

_____

_____

_____

_____

_____

A famous comedian once explained the game of football as "a cow pasture where a big group of men were trying to get hold of a funny shaped ball." In the space below write a humorous explanation of your favorite sport.

_____

_____

_____

_____

_____

_____

_____

_____

Eighteen Holes

The game of golf is played on a golf course. The course has no particular length or shape, but it usually consists of eighteen holes. Play one round of "What-What" golf by writing a definition for each golf term below.

An Unforgettable Day

It was a perfectly beautiful day on the golf course. The grass seemed greener than ever before. The ball looked especially bright, gleaming in the sunshine. I spread my feet apart, lined up my club head with the ball and lifted the club to swing at the ball. It was at that moment that I realized that the ball was not a ball at all. As my club came down against it. . . .

Complete the story. Put on your thinking cap and let your imagination soar!

_____

_____

_____

_____

_____

_____

_____

_____

_____

_____

_____

_____

_____

_____

_____

_____

_____

_____

_____

_____

GA1442

Favorite Sport Survey

Use the chart below to survey twelve of your classmates. Ask students to list their first, second, third, fourth and fifth choices of sports. Answer questions and graph your results.

Name	1st Choice	2nd Choice	3rd Choice	4th Choice	5th Choice
1.					
2.					
3.					
4.					
5.					
6.					
7.					
8.					
9.					
10.					
11.					
12.					

1. What sport was chosen first by most of the twelve students? _____

2. What sport was chosen second by most of the twelve students? _____

3. What sport was chosen third by most of the twelve students? _____

4. What sports were not chosen by anyone? _____

5. What sport do you think is the most popular in the world? How can you find the answer to this question? _____

Combine your results with those of your classmates and make a chart or graph.

The Winner!

Eldrick "Tiger" Woods' ultimate goal in 1991 was to be the youngest player ever to win the PGA title. The time is in the future. Imagine that Tiger has won the PGA and has become the youngest player ever to win it.

What might Eldrick say in his acceptance speech at the awards ceremony? What might his next goal be?

_____

_____

_____

_____

_____

_____

Have you ever won a trophy or award? Tell the reason you won the trophy or award and draw a picture of your trophy or award in the space below.

Personal Data

Name: Rosa Lee Parks
Birth Year: 1913
Birthplace: Tuskeegee, Alabama
Field: Leadership
Occupations: Former department store seamstress, civil rights leader and aide to U.S. congressman
Awards and Achievements: 1979 Spingarn Medal. Credited with starting modern civil rights movement (1955)

Biographical Information

On December 1, 1954, a tired department store seamstress boarded a downtown Montgomery, Alabama, city bus. Her feet ached from a long day's work. She took the first empty seat and breathed a sigh of relief. No sooner than she had taken her seat, the bus made another stop. Several people boarded the bus. One white man came over and stood beside the tired woman and asked her to get up and give her seat to him. The tired woman said "No." That tired woman was Rosa Parks. The bus driver became angry and shouted at her to get up, but Mrs. Parks refused to move. The bus driver left the bus and called a policeman. The policeman told Mrs. Parks that she was violating a city law that required Blacks to give up their seats to white passengers. Mrs. Parks did not budge. The policeman arrested Mrs. Parks and took her to jail. She was given a chance to make a phone call. She called a friend. The friend then contacted a young minister named Martin Luther King, Jr. The young minister called a mass meeting of Montgomery's black citizens. They organized a boycott of the city buses. This meant that no African American would ride the city buses until the laws were changed. The people chose Martin Luther King, Jr., as their leader. The boycott lasted a year. During this time Blacks walked, drove cars or took taxis to work. It was hard on everyone, but they were determined. The bus company lost a lot of money. When the year was over, African Americans were granted the right to sit in any area of the bus that had empty seats.

After this incident, African Americans went to work to change other laws that were unfair. When Mrs. Parks returned to her job, she was informed that she had been fired because of her involvement in the bus boycott. Mrs. Parks was sorry that her action had cost her her job, but she was glad that she had caused a positive change for thousands of Americans. Because of her courage to say "No!" Rosa Parks had helped change the lives of American minorities forever.

GA1442

Making Changes

Rosa Parks and the African Americans in Montgomery, Alabama, were determined to change things for a better life for all Americans. They first decided what they wanted to change, and then they decided how they were going to go about making these changes.

Here are some of the things that they wanted to change.

1. They wanted to be treated courteously by the bus driver.

2. They wanted seating to be on a first come, first serve basis.

3. They wanted the bus company to hire black bus drivers.

And here is how they were to go about making changes. They would boycott the buses. This meant that no African Americans would ride the bus until the changes were made. Think of three things that you would like to change in each category below.

School	Home	Community
1.	1.	1.
2.	2.	2.
3.	3.	3.

Select a change from each category and describe how you would go about making that change.

1. School Change _____

    How I would go about making the change _____

    _____

2. Home Change _____

    How I would go about making the change _____

    _____

3. Community Change _____

    How I would go about making the change _____

    _____

GA1442

Happy Birthday to You

In 1990 Mrs. Parks was invited to Washington, D.C., for a gala seventy-seventh birthday celebration to honor her for the leadership role that she played in the Montgomery bus boycott. You are in charge of the invitations. Design the front and inside of the card below.

Front   Inside

Write an important characteristic or trait that you think a good leader should have on each candle of Rosa Parks' birthday cake. Each tall candle stands for ten years. Each short candle stands for one year.

76

GA1442

An Encouraging Word

When Mrs. Parks made the decision not to give up her bus seat, she was not sure that she had done the right thing. She knew that in some places in the South a person could be killed for refusing to do what a white person asked her to do. But her friends encouraged and supported her. Write a letter of encouragement to Mrs. Parks in support of her decision to remain in her seat.

Dear Mrs. Parks,

_____

_____

_____

_____

_____

_____

_____

Sincerely,

Everyone needs some encouragement at one time or another. Some encouraging words to someone can mean the difference between a good day and a bad day. Write some encouraging words on the bumper stickers below.

It's Not as Bad as You Think	

GA1442

Curtains, Please!

Use the information from the story to help you write a skit called "The Rosa Parks Story." Who are the main characters?

With your teacher's permission, ask your classmates to help you act out the skit.

The Rosa Parks Story

by

_____

(your name)

Characters:

Scene I

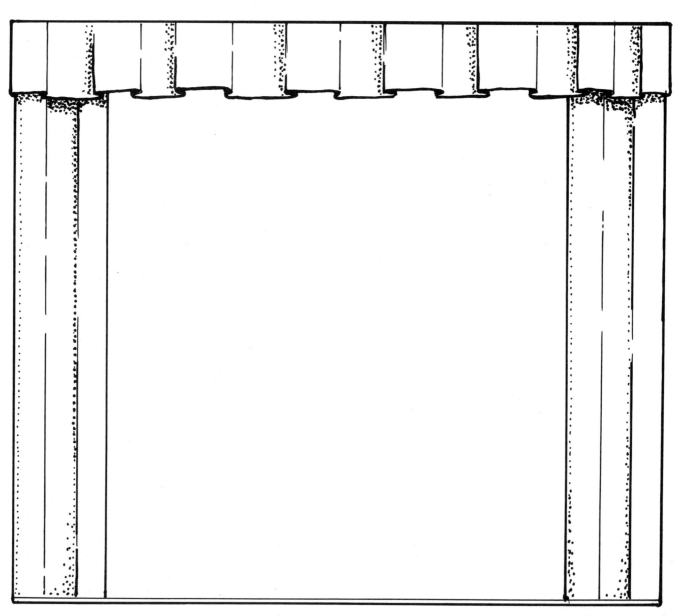

Word Power

Listed below are some words taken from the Civil Rights Era. Do you know their meanings? Write what you think each word means. Then look the word up in a dictionary or encyclopedia. How many of your meanings were correct?

1. civil rights _____

2. boycott _____

3. discrimination _____

4. marches _____

5. protest _____

6. patronize _____

7. segregation _____

8. integration _____

9. nonviolent _____

10. prejudice _____

11. freedom _____

12. bigot _____

13. unconstitutional _____

14. humiliated _____

15. inferior _____

GA1442

Personal Data

Name: Charlayne Hunter-Gault
Birth Year: 1941
Birthplace: Due West, South Carolina
Field: Media
Occupations: Broadcast journalist and writer
Awards and Achievements: Two Emmy awards; The George Foster Peabody Award, 1986; The Russell Sage Fellowship Award; Founder of the *New York Times* Harlem Bureau (1969); PBS MacNeil/Lehrer news correspondent

Biographical Information

Charlayne Hunter-Gault is a national news reporter and journalist for a PBS television network program, the *MacNeil/Lehrer Report*. As a national correspondent, she prepares and reports the news. But Charlayne has not always reported the news. She was once the news herself. It all began when Charlayne was in high school. She loved to write and do reports. In order to find an outlet for her writing, she joined her high school newspaper staff. That's when her interest in journalism began to really grow. She decided then and there that she wanted to go to college and study journalism. She had already imagined herself being a news reporter on national television. When she completed her high school education at McNeal Turner High School in Atlanta, she was selected to attend the University of Georgia at Athens. At first Charlayne was overjoyed when she received the news. Afterwards, she began to think about it. She really wanted to get a good education in journalism, but the University of Georgia was an all-white university. No other African American student had ever attended the university before. Charlayne knew what could happen and had happened when other African Americans had enrolled in all-white universities.

It took two years before the necessary preparations could be made for the two black students, Charlayne and Hamilton Holmes, to enroll at the university. Charlayne was patient because she was determined to get the best education possible in her chosen field. On a January day in 1961, her long waiting period ended, and she and Holmes enrolled in the university. They were headlines! Every major American newspaper carried the story. Charlayne was not interested in making the news; she wanted to report the news. Many students at the university were unfriendly toward Charlayne, but she was determined not to let this stop her. She had set her mind on achieving her goal, and she was determined that nothing would hold her back. During her stay at the university, Charlayne studied hard, got good grades and maintained a high academic average. She also developed a small circle of friends as students became friendlier toward her. To Charlayne, friends were important, but her studies were even more important so she spent more time with her books than her friends.

During her college summers, she went to work for an Atlanta newspaper. There she had the opportunity to practice the skills she was learning in her college classes. When Charlayne graduated from the university, she worked as a reporter for the *New Yorker* then later for the *New York Times*, and still later for a television station in Washington, D.C. Finally she was hired by Public Broadcasting's *MacNeil/Lehrer Report*. There she became nationally known, meeting and interviewing such famous persons as Desmond Tutu, President George Bush, Jesse Jackson and others. In 1988, twenty-five years after her graduation from the University of Georgia, Charlayne was invited back to the campus to give the commencement address. It was the first time in the history of the university that an African American had been selected to give the school's graduation speech. Charlayne had made news again. But this was never her intention. She had always wanted to report the news. She attributes her success to her parents and friends who supported her and who expected great things from her. She has not let them down. Charlayne Hunter-Gault is doing great things.

The Way It Was

Suppose that you are a reporter for the *The Way It Was* newspaper, and you have been designated to cover the return of Charlayne Hunter-Gault to the University of Georgia to deliver the commencement address. Write a headline and a story of her return on the newspaper below.

The Way It Was

Volume I

Journalism Words

Like most specialized professions, journalism has developed its own set of word symbols. Twenty of these are listed below. Select ten, write the meanings for them as they are used in editing and make a sentence for each word. Use dictionaries and encyclopedias if you need help. Complete the activity on the back of this page.

1. ⊙	6. stet	11. ⌗	16. copy
2. delete	7. uc	12. =	17. lead
3. ∧	8. lc	13. head	18. caret
4. ital	9. ℒ	14. -30-	19. ∪
5. # # #	10. ∧	15. byline	20. body

Word 1 _____

    Definition _____

    Sentence_____

Word 2 _____

    Definition _____

    Sentence_____

Word 3 _____

    Definition _____

    Sentence_____

Word 4 _____

    Definition _____

    Sentence_____

Word 5 _____

    Definition _____

    Sentence_____

GA1442

Things I Want

Everyone wants something and most people are willing to work hard to get what they want. So it was with Charlayne Hunter-Gault. She wanted to get a good journalism education. So she worked hard in high school and got good grades so that when the time came, she could enroll in the school of journalism at the University of Georgia.

The things that people want in life change with age. For example, at age five a child might want a teddy bear, his parents' affection and a rocking horse. Five years later, when that child is ten years old, he might want to play little league baseball, his parents' affection and a puppy.

What are some things that you want?

Your age now_____   Things you will want_____

Five years from now
Your age _____   Things you will want_____

Ten years from now
Your age _____   Things you will want_____

Twenty years from now
Your age _____   Things you will want_____

Thirty years from now
Your age _____   Things you will want_____

Compare your information with your classmates' information. Do any classmates want the same things that you want? At the same age level?

Arrange the following wants on the pyramid, putting the want that you think is most important at the number 1 position at the top of the pyramid. Put the least important want in the number 6 position at the bottom of the pyramid. Wants: peace, love, health, education, wealth, success

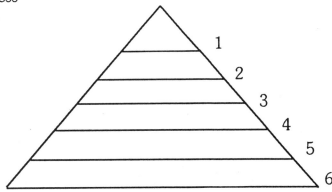

Ask Them

In her role as news correspondent, Charlayne Hunter-Gault meets and interviews many famous people. List five famous persons that you would like to meet, and write five questions that you would ask each one.

Famous person #1

1. _____
2. _____
3. _____
4. _____
5. _____

Famous person #2

1. _____
2. _____
3. _____
4. _____
5. _____

Famous person #3

1. _____
2. _____
3. _____
4. _____
5. _____

Famous person #4

1. _____
2. _____
3. _____
4. _____
5. _____

Famous person #5

1. _____
2. _____
3. _____
4. _____
5. _____

GA1442

Cover It!

Charlayne Hunter-Gault grew up in the South. She became involved in civil rights activities when she and Hamilton Holmes became the first African American students to attend the University of Georgia in Athens. She states that her experience has helped her do a good job in covering other civil rights news. How well can you cover the following civil rights news? Research each of the following civil rights topics and complete the newspaper articles below.

The Birmingham Bus Boycott	**Selma to Montgomery March**

The Assassination of Dr. Martin Luther King, Jr.

Personal Data

Name: Carl Lewis (Frederick Carlton Lewis)
Birth Year: 1961
Birthplace: Birmingham, Alabama
Field: Sports
Occupation: Track and field athlete
Awards and Achievements: Amateur Athletic Union's Award; three gold medals at World Championship Games in Helsinki, Finland, in 1983; four gold medals at the 1984 Summer Olympic Games in Los Angeles and two more gold medals at the 1988 Olympic Games

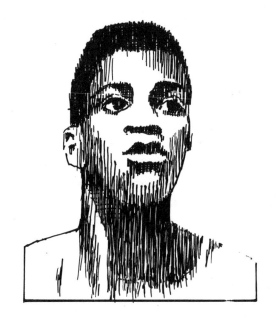

Biographical Information

On July 1, 1961, a baby boy was born to Bill and Evelyn Lewis of Birmingham, Alabama. The parents named their son Frederick Carlton Lewis. Most people who know this famous athlete today know him as Carl. When Carl was a child, his parents moved to a middle class subdivision in Willingboro, New Jersey. His mother and father, who were both high school teachers, opened a track club. When Carl was growing up in Willingboro, he showed an early interest in music. He learned to play the cello and the drums. He later became interested in track and began running for his parents' track club. When he was twelve years old, he won the long jump event in the Jesse Owens Youth Track Meet in Philadelphia. But it wasn't until high school that he really became a track star. When he graduated from high school he was considered to be the number one athlete in the United States. Carl's parents wanted their child to become all that he could become. So they encouraged him to go to college. Carl followed their advice and enrolled in the University of Houston in 1979, on an athletic scholarship. Carl was very fortunate. He trained under an expert track and field coach. In 1981 he made history for himself and the university. He participated in a track and field competition and won events in both track and field. This had never been done by any athlete in the history of the university. In the same year Carl was awarded many sporting event awards for outstanding performance in track and field. In 1984 Carl won four gold medals at the Olympic Games in Los Angeles and two more gold medals at the 1988 Olympic Games. That was quite an accomplishment. In the years that followed, Carl kept running and continued to win medals and awards. He appeared in TV commercials and advertisements for athletic equipment. A few years afterwards, Carl began to prepare himself for a second career. He began taking acting lessons. Carl Lewis is multitalented. He can sing. He is an actor. He can run fast and jump high. With all of his talents there is no telling what Carl Lewis may turn to next–but for now for Carl Lewis, running is his fun thing.

Getting to Know You

Track and field is a sport in which athletes compete in events such as running, jumping and throwing. The track events consist of races. The field events consist of jumping and throwing.

Carl Lewis was a gifted athlete in both track and field events. Several other African Americans have become famous in track and field. Select two names from the list below and write a paragraph about each one. Use encyclopedias or other reference books.

Wilma Rudolph	Bob Hayes	Ralph Metcalfe
Edwin Moses	Rafer Johnson	Otis Davis
Ralph Boston	Jesse Owens	Jackie Joyner-Kersee

Imagine you are a famous athlete. Tell what sport you are famous for and how you developed your skill in that sport.

It's All in the Family

Carl Lewis came from a very athletic family. His father was a track and football star at Tuskegee University. His mother represented the United States in the 1951 Pan American Games. Carl's older brother was a high school track star. Another brother was a professional soccer player. Carl's sister Carol was an outstanding track star. In some families it seems that similar physical traits are found throughout the family. Is this true of your family?

Complete the family tree below to help you answer this question. Add additional lines if you need them.

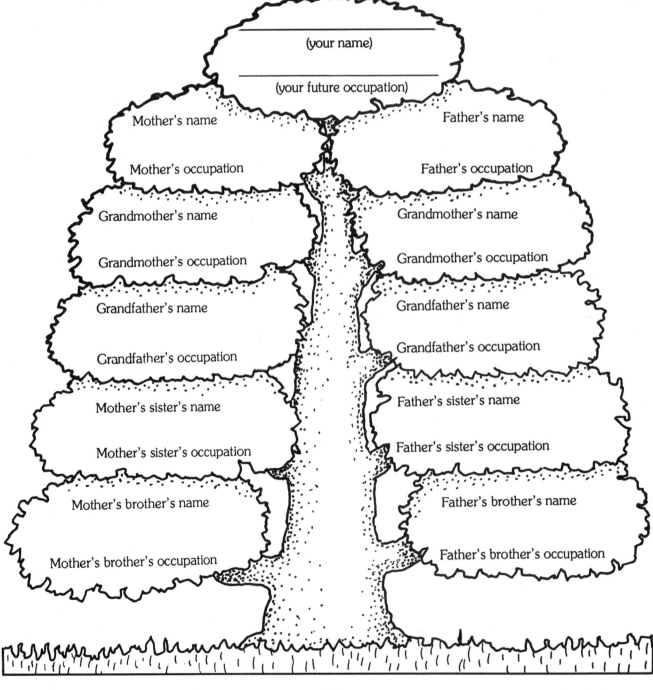

(your name)

(your future occupation)

Mother's name

Mother's occupation

Father's name

Father's occupation

Grandmother's name

Grandmother's occupation

Grandmother's name

Grandmother's occupation

Grandfather's name

Grandfather's occupation

Grandfather's name

Grandfather's occupation

Mother's sister's name

Mother's sister's occupation

Father's sister's name

Father's sister's occupation

Mother's brother's name

Mother's brother's occupation

Father's brother's name

Father's brother's occupation

GA1442

Breakfast of Champions

In addition to athletic competitions, Carl Lewis earns money from personal appearances as well as television commercials. Your company has asked you to develop a nutritious cereal for track and field athletes. On the cereal box write (1) the name of the cereal; (2) a picture of the prize inside of the box; (3) the name of the company producing the cereal; (4) ingredients, vitamins, and minerals; (5) the price of the cereal; and (6) the shape of the cereal.

Write a two-paragraph TV commerical to advertise the cereal.

Thou Shalt Not Prejudge

Carl Lewis greatly admired Jesse Owens, who showed remarkable athletic skills in the 1936 Olympics. The 1936 Olympics were held in Berlin, Germany. The German ruler Adolf Hitler believed that his countrymen were superior to the African American athletes, and he predicted that the African American athletes would not do so well in the Olympic Games. He had hoped that the results of the games would prove him right. How wrong he was! The results for African Americans in the 1936 Olympics were great. Jesse Owens won four gold medals for the 100-meter run, 200-meter run, the long jump and the 400-meter relay. John Woodruff won the 800-meter run. Cornelius Johnson set an Olympic record for the high jump. Ralph Metcalfe won a gold medal for the 400-meter relay and a silver medal for the 100-meter dash.

The African American athletes had proven Hitler wrong. Instead of congratulating them, Hitler became angry and left the stadium before all of the athletes had received their awards. The African American athletes had taught Hitler a very valuable lesson–never prejudge a person.

The word *prejudge* means "to judge someone or predict an action before it is done." The word *prejudice* comes from the word *prejudge*. There is a lot of prejudice in the world today.

You have been selected as chairman of the Committee for Better Race Relations in the World. List twenty different and unusual things that you can do to bring people closer together. Put a star beside your three best ideas.

1. _____
2. _____
3. _____
4. _____
5. _____
6. _____
7. _____
8. _____
9. _____
10. _____

11. _____
12. _____
13. _____
14. _____
15. _____
16. _____
17. _____
18. _____
19. _____
20. _____

Select one of these ideas and on the back of this page, write a plan for putting it into action.

Famous African American Olympians

Through ability, hard work and a desire to win, African American Olympians have been very successful in the Olympic Games. Read the information beside each name. Use the information to complete two or more of the following activities: (1) make a giant time line of all the events; (2) make a board game; (3) construct a quiz with true/false, multiple choice or completion questions; (4) make a word search.

1. Jesse Owens–Won four gold medals in the 1936 Olympics
2. Charles Dumas–In 1956, the first to clear 7 feet at U.S. Olympic trials
3. Wilma Rudolph–Won three gold medals in the 1960 Rome Olympics
4. Cassius Clay–Won gold medals in boxing in 1960 in Rome Olympics
5. Jackie Joyner-Kersee–Won two golds in 1988 Seoul Olympics
6. Lee Evans–Won the 400-meter run in record time in 1968 Olympics
7. George Poage–Was the first African American to participate in the 1904 Olympic Games
8. Edwin Moses–This Olympian won gold medals in 1976 in Montreal and in 1984 in Los Angeles
9. Tommie Smith and John Carlos–Raised a black-gloved fist to show unfair treatment in America at the 1968 Olympic Games
10. John Woodruff–Won 800-meter event in 1936 Berlin Olympics
11. Cornelius Johnson–Set Olympic record for high jump in 1936 Berlin Olympics
12. Eddie Tolan–Won two gold medals in 1932 Los Angeles Olympics
13. Ralph Metcalfe–Won a gold medal for the 400-meter relay and a silver for the 100-meter dash in 1936 Olympics
14. Evelyn Ashford–Broke 100-meter record at 1984 Los Angeles Olympics
15. Bob Beamon–In 1968 he stunned the world with his long jump record.
16. Florence Griffith Joyner–Set a world record in 1988 in the 100-meter and 200-meter events
17. John Taylor–Won a gold medal at the 1908 London Olympics
18. Floyd Patterson–Won the middleweight gold medal in Helsinki, Finland, in 1952
19. Alice Coachman–Won gold medal in high jump event in 1948 London Olympics
20. Rafer Johnson–Set a new decathlon record in Rome in 1960

Personal Data

Name: Coretta Scott King
Birth Year: 1927
Birthplace: Marion, Alabama
Field: Leadership
Occupation: Civil rights leader
Awards and Achievements: Named one of the most influential women (1985); speaker and fund-raiser for various black organizations; director of the Martin Luther King, Jr., Center for Social Change in Atlanta

Biographical Information

When most people think of the civil rights movement of the late fifties and early sixties, they think of Dr. Martin Luther King, Jr. Few people think of the courageous black woman who became his wife and devoted companion. Coretta Scott was born and reared on her grandfather's farm near Marion, Alabama. Her Grandpa Jeff and her Grandma Cora toiled long hours in the fields to get enough money to buy their 300-acre farm. Her grandfather and grandmother had thirteen children. One of them was Obadiah Scott, Coretta's father. In 1920 he married Bernice McMurry. Coretta's father, "Obie" as he was called, was highly respected by both black and white in the small community. They were a hard working and honest family. They raised hogs, cows, chickens, cotton and vegetables. Coretta, her sister and brother grew up helping with the farm chores. They planted, chopped and picked cotton; fed the chickens and livestock; and milked the cows. When Coretta was old enough, she attended an elementary school in the Heiberger community. The Scott children had to walk three miles to school each day, rain or shine. In the meantime, white children who lived two or three miles from their school rode a bus. The school was an unpainted wooden building with one room. Inside, a large wood-burning stove provided heat. The desks and tables were made of rough wood. One section of a wall was painted black. It was used for a blackboard. The toilets, one marked *boys* and one marked *girls*, were outside. When Coretta completed the sixth grade, she was sent to nearby Lincoln High School in Marion, Alabama. Originally the Lincoln School had been established for slave children. It had been named for Abraham Lincoln who issued the Emancipation Proclamation which declared freedom for the southern slaves. Half of the teachers at Lincoln High were white; the other half were black. The tuition was only $4.50 per year, but Coretta's mother and father had to scrimp and save to provide for her education. At Lincoln High School, Coretta became interested in music and learned to sing and play several musical instruments. After high school graduation, Coretta went to Antioch College in Yellow Springs, Ohio. There she studied to become an elementary school teacher. Her interest in music continued to grow. When she graduated from Antioch College, she was encouraged by her teachers to attend the New England Conservatory School of Music in Boston. There she met a young doctorate student named Martin Luther King, Jr., who thought right away that she had "everything I want in a wife." Soon they were married. In 1954 Martin finished his studies and came south to pastor the Dexter Avenue Baptist Church in Montgomery, Alabama. On November 17, 1954, less than three weeks after the birth of their oldest daughter, a tired woman named Rosa Parks refused to give up her seat on a city bus and the Civil Rights Movement began.

In the years that followed, Coretta and Martin were deeply involved in the civil rights movement. On many occasions Martin was jailed and beaten because of his civil rights activities. Often he was called to speak to groups and led civil rights activities in many cities across the United States. And Mrs. Coretta Scott King, his trusted companion and wife, was by his side. In April 1968, he was called to Memphis, Tennessee, where striking sanitation workers were protesting for better wages. It was at this time that Dr. Martin Luther King, Jr., was shot and killed. Since the death of her husband, Coretta has spent her time raising her children, fulfilling speaking engagements and directing activities at the Martin Luther King, Jr., Center for Social Change in Atlanta.

GA1442

A Proclamation

When Coretta Scott King finished elementary school, she attended Lincoln High School. The school was named for Abraham Lincoln who issued the Emancipation Proclamation. The Emancipation Proclamation declared freedom for all southern slaves. Use an encyclopedia or other reference books to help you learn more about the Emancipation Proclamation. Read the Emancipation Proclamation and answer these questions.

1. What date was the proclamation to be effective?
2. List all of the states and portions of states named in the proclamation.
3. How was the freedom of the slaves to be maintained?
4. What statement was made about ex-slaves serving in the armed forces of the United States?

Suppose that you had the power to issue a proclamation to encourage people to get along better with one another. What will you proclaim? Give your proclamation a name, and write it on the scroll below.

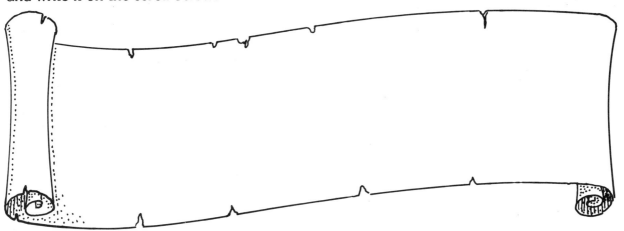

Suppose that you had the power to issue three proclamations that would be good for your school. Write the three proclamations on the scrolls below.

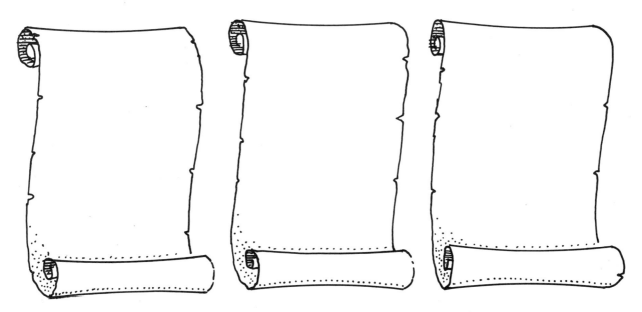

GA1442

Amendments and Rights

The writers of the Constitution could not agree on who should have the right to vote so they left it up to the individual states. During the fifty years following the adoption of the Constitution, only white men who owned land could vote. After the Civil War three amendments were passed. The thirteenth amendment abolished slavery all over the United States, the fourteenth amendment made former slaves United States citizens and the fifteenth amendment gave newly freed slaves the right to vote. Even though the Constitution had granted African Americans the right to vote, many states made it impossible to do so in Alabama by passing unfair laws.

On March 7, 1965, Coretta Scott King and her husband Dr. Martin Luther King, Jr., planned a fifty-mile march from Selma to Montgomery to bring the nation's attention to unconstitutional state voting laws. Hundreds of people joined them. Shortly after the march began, it was broken up by state troopers. Many of the marchers were harassed and beaten. This day is often referred to as "Bloody Sunday." Fourteen days later another march was planned. This time President Lyndon Johnson provided National Guard protection for the marchers. The march was a success, and on July 9, 1965, the United States Congress passed the Voting Rights Act. This law protected the right of African Americans to vote and required each state to abide by the Constitution. Research and write section 1 of the thirteenth, fourteenth and fifteenth amendments on their appropriate scrolls.

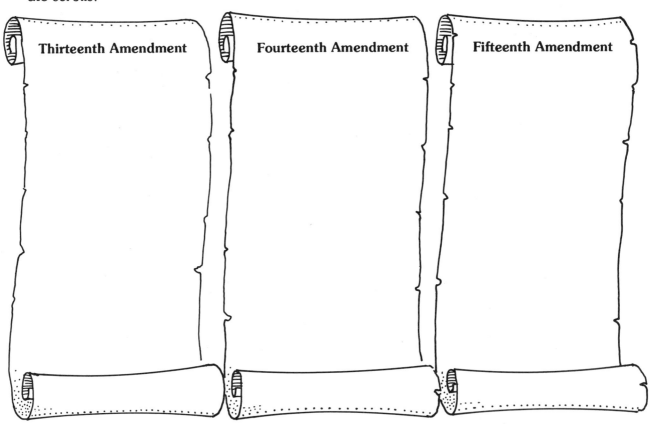

Thirteenth Amendment   Fourteenth Amendment   Fifteenth Amendment

The beginning statement of the U.S. Constitution is called the Preamble. This statement gives the reasons for establishing the Constitution. Read the Preamble and tell in your own words the reasons that are stated.

94
GA1442

Gaining the Right to Vote

When the United States ratified the U.S. Constitution in 1789, only white men could vote. In 1920 the nineteenth amendment to the Constitution was passed. It gave women the right to vote. Native American Indians were not granted the right to vote in all states until 1948. Citizens in Washington, D.C., could not vote in presidential elections until after the passage of the twenty-third amendment in 1961. In 1964 the twenty-fourth amendment abolished poll taxes, and in 1965 Congress passed the Voting Rights Act protecting the rights of African Americans to vote. The twenty-sixth amendment was passed in 1971. It gave young people eighteen years or older the right to vote. Complete the pyramid by writing in the correct information beside its correct date to show the progressive climb to today's voting rights.

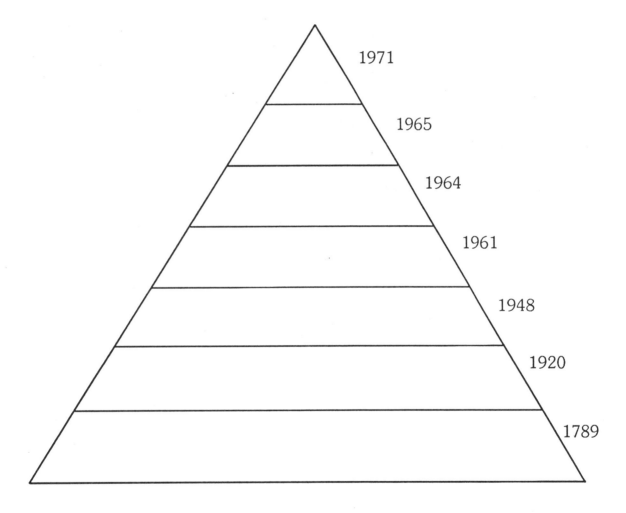

1971

1965

1964

1961

1948

1920

1789

Even though *every* U.S. citizen over the age of eighteen has the right to vote, many do not take the time to vote. Write a speech urging people to exercise their right to vote. Use the information presented above and some from other sources, too. Present your speech to the class in an interesting way.

GA1442

Nobel Peace Prize

In May 1964, Coretta Scott King traveled with her husband, Dr. Martin Luther King, Jr., to Oslo, Norway, where he received one of the world's highest honors–the Nobel Peace Prize. The prize was awarded to Dr. King for his peaceful methods of causing change. He was awarded $54,000 and a plaque. He kept the plaque, but he donated the money to the SCLC (Southern Christian Leadership Conference), an organization that helps African Americans gain their rights. Research and write some important statements about the Nobel Peace Prize on the medal below.

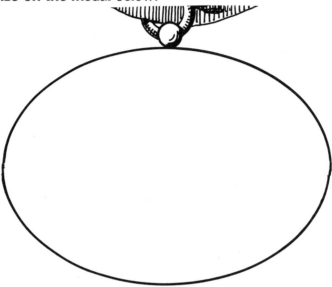

Suppose that your teacher were to give a Nobel Peace Prize in your classroom. Complete the form to show who you would nominate to receive the prize and why.

Nobel Peace Prize Nomination Form

I, _____, hereby nominate the person of
_____(your name)_____
_____ to receive the _____
_____(name of nominee)_____ _____(your grade)_____
Class Nobel Peace Prize. I nominate this person for these three reasons:

_____

_____

_____

I hereby submit this form on _____
_____(date)_____

Signed,

_____
_____(your signature)_____

GA1442

Time to Celebrate

In 1986 the government declared the third Monday in January as a national holiday to celebrate Dr. Martin Luther King, Jr.'s birthday. List things that you could do to celebrate and honor Dr. King on his birthday. Here is an example to help you get started.

1. Write a poem in memory of Dr. King.

2.

3.

4.

5.

The month of February is called Black History Month because in it falls the birthdays of two outstanding African Americans–Frederick Douglass and W.E.B. Du Bois. Research the lives of these two men. Choose one to nominate for a national holiday in February. Give reasons for your choice.

_____

_____

_____

_____

_____

_____

_____

_____

_____

_____

_____

_____

_____

_____

 GA1442

Personal Data

Name: Michael Jackson
Birth Year: 1958
Birthplace: Gary, Indiana
Field: Entertainment
Occupations: Musician, dancer, songwriter and singer
Awards and Achievements: The world's highest paid singer and entertainer. *Thriller* album made the Guinness Book of World Records as the best-selling record album of all time. It won a record-breaking eight Grammy awards (music industry's highest award).

Biographical Information

By the time Michael Jackson was thirteen years old, he had become the idol of almost every teenager in America. They chased him at airports, pasted their bedroom walls with his posters and screamed loudly at concerts. "Michael-Mania" was spreading throughout the world. The lives of the old as well as the young were being touched by Michael Jackson and his music. How did it begin?

Michael was one of Joseph and Katherine Jackson's nine children. While sitting around the house, Michael and his four brothers began to sing and play the guitar. One of his brothers suggested that they form a group and they did. The group was led by five-year-old Michael. The group was called The Jackson Five. In 1968 they signed a contract with a major recording company, and the success of The Jackson Five had begun! The Jackson Five became the most popular act in show business.

They appeared on television shows and recorded best-selling records. Their concerts and tours were sold out. In the 1970's The Jackson Five were featured in cartoons on Saturday morning television. In 1979 Michael began a solo career, recorded his first album and became one of the greatest rock singers of all time. In 1984 he produced an album called *Thriller.* It became the largest-selling album ever recorded and was entered in the Guinness Book of World Records. At the 1984 Grammy awards ceremony, Michael Jackson won eight Grammys for his *Thriller* album, more than any other entertainer had won in a single year. Michael has appeared in a major motion picture as well as rock videos. He has also written his autobiography *Moonwalk* (1988) and published a volume of poetry. In the 1990's Michael Jackson remains one of America's greatest singers, dancers and songwriters.

Produce It

More than any other performer, Michael Jackson has influenced the content and quality of music videos. Now he has hired you to produce his next music video. Complete the storyboard for the video. Draw what will be seen in the large boxes and write what will be said on the lines at the right.

_____ Storyboard

Name of Video

1. _____

2. _____

3. _____

4. _____

5. _____

GA1442

Design It

In addition to his contributions to music and video, Michael Jackson has had an impact on the fashion industry. His single sequined glove is an internationally recognized trademark. The glove is now in the Smithsonian Museum.

Design a new fashion item for Michael Jackson.

Design a new Michael Jackson poster.

Design an album cover for a new Michael Jackson album.

Creativity Boost

Michael Jackson has become one of the world's greatest singers, composers, and dancers. In order to compose, sing and perform music, one has to be creative. Being creative means to be able to produce many different and unusual ideas. Stimulate your brain and boost your creativity by completing the following activities.

1. List all the many and different things that are blue. (Use the back of this sheet.)

2. What might a pencil say to a book? _____

_____

3. What color is love? _____

4. Which is longer, Monday or Friday? Why? _____

_____

5. Complete this poem: On top of the mountain, or in the valley below_____

_____

6. List all the many different and unusual things that remind you of summer. (Use the back of this sheet.)

7. What could you do to a piano to make it a more exciting instrument? _____

_____

8. Explain this statement: "Music is a universal language." _____

_____

9. What color is hate? _____

10. Explain how singing came to be._____

_____

11. What famous musician would you like to spend a day with?_____

12. Which is quieter, gray or a piece of cotton?_____

13. List five ways to get rid of hate. (Use the back of this sheet.)

14. List all the many different and unusual things that are soft. (Use the back of this sheet.)

15. What might a set of drums say to a flute? _____

_____

GA1442

Creativity 4

Awards, Awards, Awards

Several awards are presented each year for outstanding achievement in the recording industry. The Grammy is such an award. In 1984 Michael Jackson won eight Grammy awards, more than any other entertainer at any one time in the history of the recording industry.

You are the organizer for a different kind of music award program. Complete the form below to show your plans for the presentation of this new award.

Name of award: _____

Date it will be presented (seen on television): _____

Who will host the program?_____

Who will be the guest performer to sing on the program? _____

Who will receive the award? _____

Who will sponsor the program? (What commercials will be seen?) _____

Draw a picture of the award in the space below.

The record industry also gives awards to musicians, according to the number of copies that each record sells. When 500 copies of an album have been sold, the musician gets a gold record. A musician gets a platinum record if his record sells 1 million copies and a multiplatinum record if his record sells 2 million or more. Write the name and lyrics for an award-winning platinum record below.

Name of record: _____

_____

_____

_____

_____

_____

Design an album cover for the record on the back of this sheet.

Music? Noise?

You are playing your stereo, and your mother yells, "Turn that noise off." Is music noise? When is music noise? Research, draw and label a picture of the ear. Beneath the picture tell how the ear works. Use the space below and the back of this sheet if you need more space.

On another sheet of paper write a two-paragraph report on noise pollution.

103

GA1442

Personal Data

Name: Lawrence Douglas Wilder
Birth Year: 1931
Birthplace: Richmond, Virginia
Field: Government
Occupation: Governor of the state of Virginia
Awards and Achievements: Omega Psi Phi Fraternity; the Bronze Star Medal; Trustee, Virginia Union University; Founder and Partner of the law firm of Wilder, Gregory and Martin; Spingarn Medal, 1990; the American Black Achievement Trailblazer Award, 1990

Biographical Information

When Lawrence Douglas Wilder was growing up near the governor's mansion in the Church Hill section of Richmond, Virginia, he had no idea that he would someday become the highest governing official in his state. But in November of 1989 it happened! Lawrence Wilder, the son of an insurance agent and a maid and the grandson of slaves, became the first African American to be elected governor of a U.S. state. In 1871 Pickney Benton Stewart Pinchback, an African American, served as lieutenant governor in the state of Louisiana. When the governor was impeached he became governor of Louisiana. But Douglas Wilder was the first African American to be elected to serve as governor of a state. For Douglas Wilder, the youngest of eight children born to Robert and Beulah Wilder, the climb to the top was not easy. He had come a long way from the boy who had once cleaned tables at a motel restaurant to a man who would command the business of an entire state, a job Douglas Wilder says is only possible through hard work and commitment both of which he is willing to do.

Douglas Wilder believes that a good government is one that serves its people. He also believes that the government should be there for all of the people, not just a special few. He wants more people to understand and participate in the government of the state.

Douglas Wilder's parents had wanted young Lawrence to go to college to become a mortician and open his own funeral service. But Lawrence was interested in something else. Step by step he planned a way to reach his goal. In 1951 he graduated from Virginia Union University with a B.S. degree in chemistry. In 1952 he served in the U.S. Army and was awarded a Bronze Star for bravery during the Korean War. Afterwards, he returned to Howard University in Washington, D.C., and earned a law degree. He soon became a successsful trial lawyer and opened his own law firm. In 1969 at the age of thirty-eight, he became the first African American to be elected to the Virginia state senate since 1877. He held that post for sixteen years. In 1985 he was elected lieutenant governor of Virginia. This election paved the way for his election to governor in 1989.

Lawrence Douglas Wilder was named for two outstanding African Americans, Frederick Douglass and Paul Lawrence Dunbar. Surely these two would be proud of the accomplishments of their namesake, Lawrence Douglas Wilder.

We're #1

Douglas Wilder was the first elected African American governor in the United States. Listed below are the names of twenty African Americans who were the first to achieve in a particular field or event. Read the list and find the person's italicized last name in the word search. Don't forget to look vertically, horizontally, diagonally and backwards.

1. Bill *Cosby*–won an Emmy award
2. Guion *Bluford*–astronaut
3. Mae *Jemison*–female astronaut
4. Lucius *Amerson*–elected sheriff in the South since Reconstruction
5. Debi *Thomas*–won the World Figure Skating Championship
6. Marian *Anderson*–sang at the Metropolitan Opera in New York City
7. Althea *Gibson*–tennis player who won the Wimbledon (England) and U.S. Championship
8. Emmett *Ashford*–umpire in the major leagues
9. Thurgood *Marshall*–U.S. Supreme Court justice
10. Sidney *Poitier*–won an Oscar (the Motion Picture Academy Award)
11. Gwendolyn *Brooks*–won the Pulitzer Prize for poetry
12. Henry *Blair*–received a patent for his invention of a corn planter
13. Oliver *Lewis*–jockey who won the Kentucky Derby
14. Ralph *Bunche*–won the Nobel Peace Prize
15. Richard *Hatcher*–mayor of a large American city
16. David *Dinkins*–mayor of New York City
17. W.E.B. *Du Bois*–received a Ph.D. (doctorate) degree from Harvard University
18. Booker T. *Washington*–had a stamp issued in his honor
19. George Washington *Carver*–became world famous for his research in agriculture
20. August *Wilson*–won the Pulitzer Prize for drama

```
P P E D S N O U U L Y A J A F V V
I G G K K W R Y Q R W L K M O M E
Z E I K K Q M P D J N N A E J X E
F X S R W K M K T D D I Z R X V F
U F F Q R T W N F L O E D S P W B
Y S E D O R O Z Z N X C K O W N H
B A D L C S R Q N O O F I N N W P
X A R I L T G Q T S L T S L R Y H
E M D I N A Q O B R I E L E W I S
U W W P A K H Y T E E E H C N U B
B N E C K L I S R D F C A R V E R
M H K U L F B N R N T H P H J I S
J N O T G N I H S A W O D E R N J
T T Y C V C E I H S M R M M V J Z
L H Z J U E O C Q H O I I Z E Q J
B L O I H B I C V F S K O O R B Z
U G P M U E V F U O U Y G P L S V
N P V D A C W L N R C H F D B L X
J G O N O S B I G D E B N W R X V
```

Can you find these names?
Washington
Dinkins
Ashford
Jemison
Du Bois
Gibson
Blair
Marshall
Hatcher
Amerson
Wilson
Bunche
Thomas
Cosby
Anderson
Poitier
Bluford
Carver
Brooks
Lewis

GA1442

Trailblazer

In 1990, Douglas Wilder was awarded the Trailblazer Award. The Trailblazer Award is presented to the African American who is the first to excel in a particular area or field of endeavor. In the space below draw your version of the Trailblazer Award.

A genie has appeared before you. She tells you that she can grant you a wish so that you can be the first ever to do something. What do you want to be the first to do? Tell her all about it in the space below.

_____

_____

_____

_____

Name and design an award to be presented to you for this first ever achievement.

Name of award: _____

This is what my award will look like:

African American Hall of Fame

Pretend that the following African Americans have just been selected for the African American Hall of Fame. Beneath the name in each window write two or three statements telling why you think that person's name should be included in the African American Hall of Fame. Use encyclopedias and other reference books if you need help.

**African American
Hall of Fame**

George Washington Carver	W.C. Handy	Booker T. Washington
Sidney Poitier	Alex Haley	Duke Ellington
Oprah Winfrey	Shirley Chisholm	Michael Jackson
Percy Julian	Mary McLeod Bethune	Dr. Martin Luther King, Jr.

Hometown Hall of Fame

List ten African Americans, either in your hometown or nationally, that you would nominate to be included in the African American Hall of Fame. Complete a nominating form for each person giving the name of the person and the reason for your nomination.

Name: _____	Name: _____	Name: _____	Name: _____
Reason: _____	Reason: _____	Reason: _____	Reason: _____

Name: _____	Name: _____	Name: _____	Name: _____
Reason: _____	Reason: _____	Reason: _____	Reason: _____

Name: _____	Name: _____
Reason: _____	Reason: _____

Creativity 5

Tribute

In 1990, *Ebony* magazine paid tribute to many outstanding African Americans during its twelfth annual American Black Achievement Award (ABBA) ceremony, held at the Celebrity Theater in Hollywood, California. At the ceremony Lawrence Douglas Wilder received the Trailblazer Award. The Trailblazer Award is presented to the African American who has become the first to achieve excellence in a particular endeavor. Douglas Wilder received the award for becoming the first African American to be elected governor in the United States. Read the information in the chart and complete the activities that follow.

Name of Award	Award Given For	Name of Recipient	Reason for Receiving the Award
Ebony Career Achievement Award	Outstanding achievement	Quincy Jones	For his achievement in composing and arranging music
Martin Luther King, Jr., Award for Public Service	Outstanding achievement in government or community service	Maynard Jackson Andrew Young	They won the right to host the 1996 Olympic Games in Atlanta.
Jackie Robinson Award for Athletics	Most outstanding achievement in athletics	Art Shell	NFL's first black head coach
The Business and Professional Award	Outstanding accomplishment in business	Kenneth Chenault	For his achievement in business
The Dramatic Arts Award	Outstanding accomplishment in film, theater and television	Morgan Freeman	As an actor in the film *Driving Miss Daisy*
The Fine Arts Awards	Outstanding achievement in art, classical music, dance and literature	Kathleen Battle	For her accomplishment in recording
The Music Award	The most creative accomplishment by a performer in a live appearance	Bobby Brown	For his achievement as a recording artist, performer and composer
The Religion Award	The most outstanding accomplishment in the field of religion	Rev. Dr. Joseph Lowery	For his accomplishment as a minister
The International Trailblazer Award	For trailblazing achievements on the international level	Nelson Mandela	For his role in the fight to end apartheid (segregation) In South Africa
The Thurgood Marshall Education Award	For the most outstanding contribution to the field of education	Dr. Frederick Humphries	

The following persons were nominated for different awards even though they did not receive an award. Read the nominees and reasons and determine for what field each was nominated. Write your answer in the blanks.

_____ 1. M.C. Hammer–For his accomplishment as a rap music artist

_____ 2. Isiah Thomas–For his achievement as the Most Valuable Player of the National Basketball Association (NBA)

_____ 3. Denzel Washington–For his award-winning performance in the movie *Glory*

_____ 4. Sister Cora Billings–For her achievement in becoming the first black nun to head a parish in the United States

_____ 5. August Wilson–For his achievement in writing his Pulitzer Prize-winning play *The Piano Lesson*.

If you had to present an award for the two categories below for this year, who would you nominate? Give your reasons.

The Martin Luther King, Jr., Award

Name of person: _____

Reason:_____

_____

The Music Award

Name of person: _____

Reason: _____

_____

Create your own version of a trophy for each of the categories listed below.

The Religion Award

The Music Award

The Jackie Robinson Award

GA1442

Speak Up

"Johnny get up," mother's voice rings out. You turn over, pull the cover up around your neck and announce, "Coming in a minute." Your day has begun and you have used the one major tool of communication that connects you to every person that you will encounter throughout the day. That tool is speech. Every day you talk. All day you talk. En route to school you talk. Between classes you talk. Even in class you talk.

Can you imagine life without speech? We develop our speech as a baby and continue to use it for the rest of our lives. The average adult person speaks over 4800 words per day. Some people continue to develop their skills and become very good speakers, others, not so good. Douglas Wilder is an eloquent speaker. As governor of Virginia, he is in great demand across the nation. Sometimes he delivers several speeches in one day. Being able to speak well is a great advantage to those serving in public office. Part of their job is to be able to communicate their ideas to others.

"Practice makes perfect" is a true statement when it is referring to speech. The more you practice, the better speaker you will become. Select a topic from the list below and prepare and deliver a two-minute speech.

school	television	major disaster	homework
summer vacations	books	airplane trips	study skills
fads and fashions	music	overseas travel	superstitions

Follow these steps to help you prepare and deliver your speech.

1. Select and narrow your topic.
2. Gather information on your topic.
3. Adjust your speech to your audience.
4. Outline your speech to determine what you will say first, second, and so on.
5. Practice your speech.

When you are ready, get your teacher's permission and give your speech to the class.

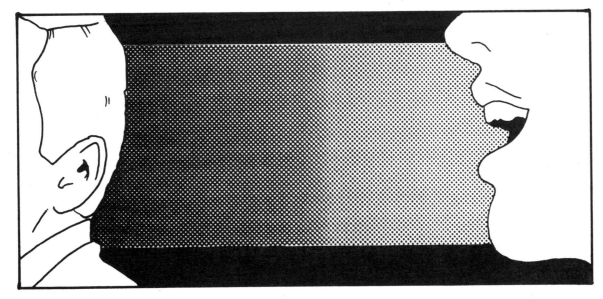

GA1442

Tourist Attraction

Congratulations, the governor has appointed you tourism director of your state. As tourism director it is your job to obtain federal funds to increase tourism to your state. In order to do this, you must testify before a congressional committee to tell why your state deserves the funds. Below prepare a convincing speech about the tourist attractions in your state. Include other information such as the state's nickname, capital, location, population, chief products, state motto and state song, libraries and museums, universities and colleges, parks and recreation areas, annual events and celebrations and any other information that you think will convince the congressional committee that your state deserves additional federal funds for tourism. Have your classmates serve as members of the Congressional Committee, and present your information to them. Use your information to design and make a colorful brochure about your state.

Name of my state:_____

State's Nickname	
Capital	
Location	
Population	
State Song and State Motto	
Chief Products	
Libraries and Museums	
Universities/Colleges	
Parks and Recreation Areas	
Annual Events and Celebrations	

GA1442

Personal Data

Name: Spike Lee
Birth Year: 1957
Birthplace: Atlanta, Georgia
Fields: Art and entertainment
Occupations: Filmmaker and actor
Awards and Achievements: He writes, directs and stars in his own films.

Biographical Information

Spike Lee was the oldest of five children born to Billy Lee, a jazz musician, and Jacquelyn Lee, a teacher of art. Both of Spike's parents were college graduates. After Spike was born, his father moved the family to Chicago and then New York. Right from the start movies were a part of Spike's life. When he was a small child, his mother took him to museums, plays and movies. He learned at an early age to appreciate such events. His father exposed him to jazz music. Whenever he played at jazz clubs, he took Spike with him. When Spike graduated from high school in 1975, he enrolled in Morehouse College in Atlanta, just as his father and grandfather had done before him. In college he participated in a variety of extracurricular activities such as writing for the school newspaper and working as a disc jockey for a local radio station. It was here that his interest in filmmaking began to grow. He undertook amateur filmmaking using his Super 8 movie camera. After college graduation in 1979, Spike worked at the Columbia Pictures Studios in Burbank, California, for a summer and returned to New York to begin work toward a master's degree in filmmaking.

In 1982 he completed the master's program and began his career as an independent filmmaker. His first films met with obstacles and disappointments, but Spike overcame these problems. He had a fierce determination to succeed. His determination was not without its rewards. On August 8, 1986, one of his films met with great success. It grossed over seven million dollars. Due to the overwhelming success of this film and two others that followed, Spike Lee became a notable filmmaker. In the 1990's two of his best films, *Do the Right Thing* and *Jungle Fever*, became big box office hits.

Spike Lee was born Shelton Jackson Lee. His mother named him Spike when he was a toddler, and the name has stuck with him. Perhaps it reflects all the toughness, persistence and patience that was necessary for his success. Fame and fortune have not changed his life-style. He lives in a sparsely furnished apartment and uses either his bike or the subways as transportation. He does not own a car or have a driver's license.

Lights, Camera, Action

A new Spike Lee movie is in the making. It will feature the life of one of the famous African Americans listed below. Before the film can be made, a script has to be written. The playwright must have correct biographical information.

Select one of the names and write a biographical sketch. Then use the information to write a one-act play or skit about that person's life.

1. George Washington Carver

2. Charles Richard Drew

3. Harriet Tubman

4. Marian Anderson

5. Wilma Rudolph

6. Jesse Jackson

7. Garrett Morgan

8. Coretta Scott King

Subject: _____

Biographical Sketch: _____

_____

_____

_____

_____

_____

Movie Reviewer

You are a movie reviewer for the local paper. List five good movies that you have seen recently, either at the theater, at home or on television. Write the name of each movie in a marquee below and write a two-paragraph summary beneath each title.

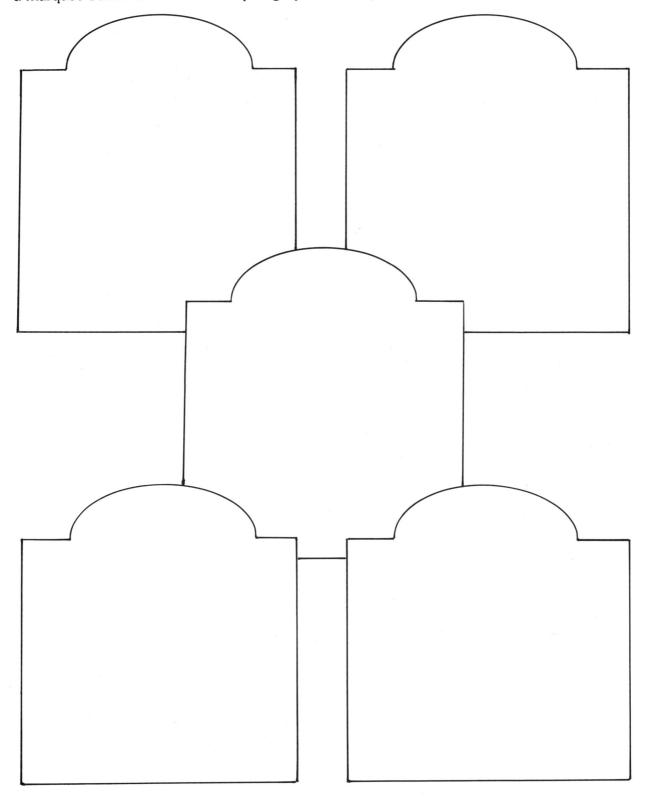

GA1442

Movie Words

When was the last time you saw a good movie? Every week millions of people either go to the movies or rent movie videos and watch them in their homes. Movies are a big industry. A regular full-length movie costs several million dollars to make and requires hundreds of skilled workers. The job titles of these workers and some terms that are used in the movie industry are hidden in the puzzle. Can you find all thirty of them? Be sure to look vertically, horizontally, diagonally and backward. When you have found them all, use an encyclopedia to look up all of the starred words to find out what people in these positions do.

```
A  J  P  W  R  M  Z  A  C  T  R  E  S  S  U  U  J  C  J  V  H
L  Q  X  T  I  E  D  U  B  B  I  N  G  D  N  L  R  B  V  K  V
I  K  J  B  C  R  S  O  P  J  Q  O  A  O  C  Z  E  T  T  N  B
Q  E  K  I  V  V  D  O  J  S  J  H  U  A  L  A  H  R  D  M  P
I  C  T  I  M  D  D  C  P  I  T  P  V  Z  Z  U  P  G  M  L  K
N  P  H  N  S  M  F  I  L  M  R  O  T  I  D  E  A  Q  W  V  E
B  N  K  G  D  X  Z  H  L  Y  O  R  R  G  Y  H  R  N  W  H  K
U  Y  Z  Y  A  L  P  N  E  E  R  C  S  Y  N  M  G  R  S  V  O
Y  M  S  M  W  B  U  D  O  L  L  I  E  S  B  I  O  E  S  N  R
M  P  J  W  C  Y  Y  T  D  A  N  M  M  A  R  O  T  C  A  P  E
R  E  M  R  O  F  R  E  P  I  Q  O  A  R  T  U  A  O  H  G  N
P  Z  I  J  T  J  F  S  R  U  R  C  R  T  X  V  M  R  O  E  G
D  T  L  E  G  C  T  C  O  J  K  E  F  X  G  T  E  D  D  H  I
S  H  R  Z  A  I  P  R  P  T  S  A  C  E  W  T  N  I  S  K  S
Q  G  T  J  C  S  H  I  E  F  N  O  I  T  A  M  I  N  A  E  E
T  P  S  K  W  U  O  P  R  E  T  I  R  W  O  P  C  G  H  L  D
K  Z  D  U  O  M  E  T  T  R  E  C  U  D  O  R  P  S  U  O  E
U  M  C  J  G  D  T  F  Y  P  A  A  I  L  F  Z  U  E  K  R  J
J  T  K  Z  F  M  Q  V  X  H  A  X  U  R  A  R  E  M  A  C  N
```

Can you find these words?

*cinematographer	music	camera	dubbing
screenplay	cast	extras	frames
recording	storyboard	actor	*editor
*director	clapstick	role	writer
*producer	performer	microphone	film
dollies	*designer	animation	set
rushes	*composer	shooting	
script	actress	property	

GA1442

Moviemaker

Imagine that Spike Lee has hired you to help in the production of his next big movie. He is looking for a good movie idea that will make a smash hit at the box office.

Write titles for five good movies below.

1.

2.

3.

4.

5.

Select your best idea and write a description of it telling what the new movie will be about.

In this movie_____

_____

_____

_____

_____

Below draw a poster showing one scene from the movie.

GA1442

And the Winner Is . . .

A film festival is an event in which new movies are shown, and awards and prizes are given for the best pictures and performances. It is also a time when distributors look for new films that they think will make a profit. The London and New York City festivals are the most popular film festivals. The best-known film award is the Academy Award or Oscar. The Oscar is a gold-plated bronze statue. It received its name in 1931, when an academy librarian said it looked like her Uncle Oscar.

In his final year as a graduate student, Spike Lee wrote, produced and directed a movie called *Joe's Bed-Stuy Barbershop,* a film about ghetto life. His movie was so good that it won a student Oscar.

Oscars are given in many different categories. Best Actor, Best Actress, Best Supporting Actor, Best Supporting Actress, Best Director and Best Picture are a few of the most celebrated awards.

In 1963 Sidney Poitier became the first African American actor to win an Oscar. Use an encyclopedia to research and complete the data card on this famous actor.

Name:

Birth Year:

Birthplace:

Occupation:

Awards and Achievements:

Facts About His Life:
   Name of movie for which he won an Academy Award (Oscar):

   Other movies in which he has starred:

Personal Data

Name: Bryant Gumbel
Birth Year: 1948
Birthplace: New Orleans, Louisiana
Field: Television media
Occupation: Broadcast journalist
Awards and Achievements: Co-anchor of NBC's *Today Show*; Edward R. Murrow Award; New York Brotherhood Award, 1976; Emmy Award, 1977; Emmy Golden Mike Award 1978 and 1979

Biographical Information

Bryant Gumbel is called one of the best morning news interviewers of all time. In 1982 he became the first African American to cohost a major morning talk show. He began his climb to fortune and fame as a writer with a black sports magazine. His interest in sports began at an early age. He loved sports. He loved the way his dad played baseball with him and his brothers. As he grew up his interest in sports continued. After attending elementary and high school, he enrolled in college where he played baseball and football. After college graduation, Bryant felt that he wanted to be a sportscaster on television. He went to New York City. He couldn't get a job in sports broadcasting, so he worked in a paper bag factory. After a year Bryant became disappointed and quit his job. For a time he didn't have a job. He barely had money for rent and food. Then one day he sent in an article to a black sports magazine and was hired. Bryant was glad to have a job again. In eight short months Bryant worked his way to editor in chief. When he was twenty-three years old, he was hired by a Los Angeles TV station as a sportscaster. It was what he had always wanted to do. He would go to New York City on weekends to broadcast football, baseball and basketball games for NBC Sports, and then return to his job in Los Angeles after the weekend. In 1980 Bryant left the sportcasting field and signed with NBC as cohost of the *Today Show*. On the *Today Show* Bryant Gumbel not only reports the news but also interviews many of the people who are in the news. His relaxed and confident manner–whether speaking with an ordinary citizen or a head of state–is admired by many in the industry. He has received many important awards, medals and plaques.

Bryant Gumbel has come a long way from sportswriter to co-anchor of the *Today Show*. When he is not busy with the show, he relaxes with his family in their apartment in New York City, their vacation place in the surburbs or his home in Los Angeles. When he cannot be found in any of those places, he can probably be found on the golf course, still exercising his love for sports.

Creativity 1

Back to the Future

In 1986 Bryant Gumbel was named "Best Morning TV News Interviewer" by more than 1000 other journalists. Bryant states that his job is a "seven-day-a-week job" in which he spends a great deal of time reading, researching, listening and absorbing.

The time is the future. You are a successful broadcast journalist. Suddenly, without warning, you find yourself flying through a time tunnel back in time. In order to get back to the future, you must complete each activity along the way. Write your answer beneath each question. Use the names in the name bank and encyclopedia if you need help.

Name Bank

Matthew Henson   Garrett Morgan   George Washington Carver
Benjamin Banneker   Jean Baptiste Point Du Sable   Daniel Hale Williams
Ronald McNair   Bill Pickett   James Weldon Johnson
Percy Julian

Begin

1. Name the African American scientist who invented the traffic light and a gas mask.

2. Who made hundreds of products from peanuts and potatoes?

3. Name the African American astronaut who died in the 1986 Challenger space shuttle explosion.

4. He was a famous African American rock star. Name him.

5. He founded the city of Chicago. Name him.

6. He was a mathematician and astronomer who surveyed the city of Washington, D.C.

7. He performed the first successful open-heart surgery. Name him.

8. He was the first to set foot on the North Pole.

9. He invented drugs to prevent and treat glaucoma and cancer.

10. He wrote the Negro National Anthem. Name him.

Back to the Future!

GA1442

Travel Plans

Sometimes news or sports correspondents have to travel to different parts of the world to report or comment on events. You have been hired to cover a news event in a foreign country. What country will you visit?_____

Use an encyclopedia, almanac or other reference books to write information on the topics below.

1. Location of country _____

2. Type of government_____

3. Industries _____

4. Currency _____

5. Language(s) _____

6. Education_____

7. Chief crops _____

8. Life expectancy_____

9. Religion _____

10. Tourist attractions_____

Combine all the information to write an interesting report for the evening news. Write your report below. Use the back of this sheet if you need more space.

_____

_____

_____

_____

_____

_____

_____

_____

_____

_____

Creative Story Starter

As a writer of feature stories one has to be able to write interesting stories. Make and use the creative story starter to write an interesting story.

List five animals in the first column. Your list can include imaginary animals, prehistoric animals, household pets or wild animals. List five places in the middle column—in a forest, a city, a desert, etc. The third column should include actions such as running, sawing, fixing a light switch, etc.

After you have completed each column, use a die or spinner to choose an item from each list. Combine an animal from the first column with a place from the second column and an action from the third column to write an interesting feature story. Use the back of this page if you need more space. Give your story a title and make it fun to read.

Animals	Places	Actions
1. _____	_____	_____
2. _____	_____	_____
3. _____	_____	_____
4. _____	_____	_____
5. _____	_____	_____

My Story Title:_____

_____

_____

_____

_____

_____

_____

_____

_____

_____

_____

_____

GA1442

Take a Break

Television commercials are an inevitable part of network TV talk shows. They give the talk show host and guest a chance to relax from the watchful eyes of the television camera, and they also help pay the broadcasting bill.

People who write commercials are always trying to think of clever ways to sell products. They use gimmicks to make us want to buy products. They show us the fastest cars, the greatest skateboard, and the hottest styles to make us feel that we must have their products. A copywriter writes the script or words for a commercial. An artist designs a storyboard. The storyboard is a set of drawings and sentences that tell the action that the camera will film while the script is spoken.

Create a thirty-second commercial on the storyboard below for a new type of ice cream. What is the name of the ice cream? What does it taste like? Have a friend help you time your commercial.

_____ **Storyboard**
Name of Video

1. _____
   _____
   _____
   _____

2. _____
   _____
   _____
   _____

3. _____
   _____
   _____
   _____

4. _____
   _____
   _____
   _____

5. _____
   _____
   _____
   _____

GA1442

Fact or Opinion?

As a successful news interviewer and talk show host, Bryant Gumbel has to know the difference between facts and opinions. Do you know the difference between the two words? A fact is a true statement: The sun is 93 million miles away from the earth, or 12 inches makes a foot. You can check in a book to prove whether a fact is true or false. An opinion is what someone thinks about something. "Pizza is not good for you." Opinions usually use words like *think, worst, bad, better, should, perhaps, believe.*

Read the sentences below. Write *F* if the sentence is a fact. Write an *O* beside the sentence if it is an opinion.

      _____ 1. Perhaps we should go now.

      _____ 2. It is a rainy day.

      _____ 3. There are nine justices on the Supreme Court.

      _____ 4. I like soccer better than football.

      _____ 5. There are seven days in a week.

Write five facts about your school such as the name of the school, where it is located and how many teachers there are.

Write five opinions about your school. Opinions might include what you like best about your school, what you think about the food in the cafeteria or what you would change about your school.

My Five Facts

1. _____
2. _____
3. _____
4. _____
5. _____

My Five Opinions

1. _____
2. _____
3. _____
4. _____
5. _____

Use the facts and opinions to write a news report or article about your school.

Information Update Sheet

Today's Date _____   Name of Person _____

Birth Year _____   Field(s) _____

Occupation _____

Is this person alive today? _____

If he/she is alive, what is his/her age? _____

Research, using most recent encyclopedia, world almanac, magazines or newspapers, the most recent awards and achievements of this person. Write this information below.

_____

_____

_____

Write additional interesting information that you can find out about the person below.

_____

_____

_____

Name some more recent African Americans who are famous in the same field or occupation as this person. _____

_____

_____

_____

What will be the date thirty years from today's date? Month_____Date _____
Year_____
Write about your hopes and dreams for thirty years in the future. Use the space below and the back of this sheet if you need more space. _____

_____

_____

_____

_____

_____

GA1442

African American Scientists and Inventors

The last names of twenty African American scientists and inventors are hidden in the puzzle below. Can you find them all? Be sure you look vertically, horizontally, backward and diagonally.

```
U F W Y C N J B T I S T E J R B K T
A A S V S U G H U W P T B H T C D Y
Z C T Z W O G E E A B A B E R E B G
O A J U L I A N B J W E G J Y J W W
B Q N Y R U K N T J L L Q E E L I Y
E X K W D E T T D X T V G M K M R J
H T L W O P K I A W K R I A C X M S
B P S S E R Q E O W J S S O H C B T
Z L Y Y L Y B Q N F O W D M K S O P
V U V T F O R T E N L C H O K J B Y
W E R E G I L E Z T A M D B O V L D
Q U X U E I L L I R T B R N G W B Q
K H O L O P L P R E I G E B V L D A
L L K Q M Z S U Q V M S W E P W M X
D R A E B O T X R R E P J J G P A J
D P T C U H R W L A R L H X O I N U
J C N V E K O G L C B U N D H R U O
J T I R M F Q W A D E Q M H G X J G
M R S V R L Y H H N P Y P F T E S P
```

George Carruthers	Jan E. Matzeliger	Norbert Rillieux
Benjamin Banneker	Mae Jemison	Lewis Latimer
Louis Wright	Lewis Temple	Garrett Morgan
Percy Julian	James Forten	George W. Carver
Dorothy Brown	Granville Woods	Elijah McCoy
Frederick Jones	Andrew Beard	Lloyd Hall
Charles R. Drew	Joseph Lee	

How many additional names can you add to this list? Select a name from the list and write an information paper on that person.

African American
Civil Rights Leaders

The last names of twenty African American civil right leaders are hidden in the puzzle below. Can you find them all? Be sure you look vertically, horizontally, backward and diagonally.

```
E  L  C  Q  Y  W  E  L  M  A  R  O  M  G  E  Y  M
Z  V  A  Z  F  K  U  V  L  X  Z  Y  G  H  H  Z  K
M  H  B  N  B  G  Z  N  O  W  F  O  H  T  A  K  S
U  Q  P  Y  Q  L  N  B  K  H  D  U  A  L  Y  E  C
N  T  J  L  H  Y  P  C  A  I  S  N  I  K  L  I  W
X  Q  U  U  O  S  X  F  M  T  R  G  O  M  F  X  L
P  M  L  T  M  D  H  E  T  E  W  O  X  B  I  K  J
G  P  F  B  C  E  N  T  B  L  R  G  J  N  U  Q  P
S  E  N  O  S  K  C  A  J  O  A  E  N  Q  N  P  Q
H  B  F  Y  H  Q  H  L  R  R  C  O  D  S  H  X  C
F  O  T  I  T  Z  R  B  V  S  H  A  H  I  W  R  J
N  Q  O  N  F  G  R  E  G  O  R  Y  J  S  T  I  V
A  V  F  K  N  U  Y  R  M  P  R  E  M  L  J  H  N
A  C  I  L  S  I  E  T  K  A  B  X  V  L  S  P  M
Q  N  G  T  Y  G  L  D  I  R  H  V  L  E  X  P  H
G  Z  I  U  Z  T  D  J  W  K  R  Q  T  W  Z  X  P
O  N  E  M  B  I  W  G  U  S  M  A  M  R  M  S  B
E  R  L  Z  J  E  E  H  T  I  B  I  M  A  R  H  F
```

Ralph Abernathy	A. Phillip Randolph	James Meredith
Mary Talbert	Roy Wilkins	Jesse Jackson
Dick Gregory	Marcus Garvey	Baynard Rustin
Fannie Lou Hamer	Medgar Evers	Ida B. Wells
Walter White	Whitney Young	Daisy Bates
Rosa Parks	John Jacob	Benjamin Hooks
Julian Bond	Martin Luther King, Jr.	

How many additional names can you add to this list? Select a name from the list and write an information paper on that person.

GA1442

African American Abolitionists

The last names of twenty African American abolitionists are hidden in the puzzle below. Can you find them all? Be sure you look vertically, horizontally, backward and diagonally.

```
Y L Y A E B T F D J H I L A A Q M B N Z
W X P V U C E M C G F F F E N Y A I G Z
I C E S N C H E M I I W A R D N O M E R
E U G A K U S L M Z Z W T O E E Y M O L
E R E L S O V N O C X F U N R O L F S I
F N N X C L E H S C V G R T S P T A D R
Q C J X L L T Y J Q L J N E O D I V N B
O H A L L S T E W A R T E O N X T S B Y
K W S A I E S S S N L S R I S M O R C J
X I X V T L W S N E T R O F T N S O E P
M U R C S G Y Z M L W R F S C N E Q A Q
R U T G Y G T M Z L L E E V E D N H U D
P G P D A U U E E Y V D N X K V O O W Q
W A L K E R X R F Y P G G L Y U J W D K
F B F M C Q N C X H R M Z P S R S T N Y
E B E T Q F G E L S O E B C A T K Q K A
A I N B Q P I D T K R Z R C D I U X D T
F B G G X F Z B K P B F L D N K Y D X W
```

Frederick Douglass	Osborne Anderson	Maria Stewart
David Ruggles	Alexander Crummel	David Walker
Nat Turner	Charles Remond	Robert Purvis
Josiah Henson	Henry Garnet	Charlotte Forten
Martin Delany	William Still	John Jones
Richard Allen	Samuel Ward	William Nell
Prince Hall	Henry Bibb	

How many additional names can you add to this list? Select a name from the list and write an information paper on that person.

African American Pioneers

The last names of twenty African American pioneers are hidden in the puzzle below. Can you find them all? Be sure you look vertically, horizontally, backward and diagonally.

```
T Q Y U G W R W V S S M W M M U V V V P K
O J B W J W U Q J J E K C A L F I D X U Y
I I C W R N H B L N H D P H H B R X N E B
X L I M W V K I P X G Z V A Y G E O F N M
L S Z Q P Y U U P K R O N R T Z R P I A G
R U S Z K D E F M P R F X B O O P K I L R
K A D D S J U H I A E F F A O B O K Q L U
K O M H K R X S A E S R W T J A M Q C P M
E C H X Y W S L A K L O F T N Y V I F N B
J G N Y Z M J I Q B O D N U F E O U M F C
F M Q S H M S D L D L S S C J C G U O I X
T T H O H I R E S N B E C K W O U R T H T
S Z B G A K Z O F O X D Q S T N D F E J E
E S T E B A N W A S H I N G T O N D F E A
E J T N O T G N I N N E P X E S R Q U E N
M O H V W Y L G N H W L G E K N Z D V X E
W T Z F U U T I S O O X U K C E U R U D Q
A F O B K W N U K J R L C V I H V M D M E
F Q V G P E B N V Z B W Y Y P D Q Q D K H
```

William Leidesdorff   James Pennington   George Washington
James Beckwourth   James Johnson   Crispus Attucks
Bill Pickett   Carter Woodson   Jean B. Du Sable
William Whipper   *Abraham   *Esteban
Matthew Henson   Paul Cuffee   Mary Fields
Biddy Mason   Clara Brown   Nancy Green
Barney Ford   George Bush

How many additional names can you add to this list? Select a name from the list and write an information paper on that person.

*No last name given

African American Entertainers

The last names of twenty African American entertainers are hidden in the puzzle below. Can you find them all? Be sure you look vertically, horizontally, backward and diagonally.

```
R  J  J  E  B  M  E  C  V  P  P  E  S  Y  L  D  T
W  T  E  H  G  S  T  C  L  C  O  L  D  T  B  F  Z
G  V  Y  F  C  I  I  N  I  I  N  Q  D  S  Z  H
Q  F  C  G  V  X  J  L  K  S  T  O  Z  X  J  K  D
J  T  I  H  J  P  Y  Q  A  E  I  S  A  E  Z  F  C
Q  Y  O  T  V  B  X  E  H  S  E  K  H  Y  I  P  W
A  I  V  N  J  V  A  J  R  C  R  C  N  R  R  O  C
N  K  J  K  I  B  N  F  S  F  L  A  B  E  L  L  E
R  E  N  R  A  W  I  P  A  T  N  J  M  L  H  A  A
V  T  J  K  S  I  V  W  V  A  O  I  O  L  V  P  R
J  D  E  X  E  L  V  O  X  O  T  B  W  A  D  E  K
A  R  X  Q  L  S  F  N  C  C  S  N  C  H  V  D  P
V  I  F  C  R  O  Y  D  H  U  U  W  M  O  O  R  E
Q  C  J  V  A  N  D  E  R  S  O  N  L  R  S  W  E
X  U  F  R  H  R  L  R  L  T  H  G  I  N  K  B  G
T  C  O  H  C  L  H  I  H  I  X  V  X  E  O  E  Y
W  J  R  R  J  E  F  Y  Z  V  A  R  M  L  X  N  V
```

Wynton Marsalis	Arthur Mitchell	Marian Anderson
Sidney Poitier	Patti LaBelle	Whitney Houston
Ray Charles	Michael Jackson	Oprah Winfrey
Gladys Knight	Nancy Wilson	Danny Glover
Malcolm-Jamal Warner	Stevie Wonder	Melba Moore
Josephine Baker	Lena Horne	Alvin Ailey
Bill Cosby	Arsenio Hall	

How many additional names can you add to this list? Select a name from the list and write an information paper on that person.

African American Women

The last names of twenty African American women are hidden in the puzzle below. Can you find them all? Be sure you look vertically, horizontally, backward and diagonally.

```
A W L U Y N K A V Y U T R G I Q
T T E N R A B B O W S E R P K I
S T H O Y M T U I T H D D M W I
K Q Q L L E R R E T V H R F C V
R J Y E S L N R A X D T A T J E
D V W U Y O Z O S W H U W Y D Q
A I A U T C R U H U E R E G H T
S F J Z R N C G S A T T T R F A
D O E G F B A H F O M U S A G I
K U J N Z Y V S D C B E R Y L I
T G M U M X H D A M Y C J F C Q
U I L T X U M R A E E I B G Q Z
E U P C X O Y N D F L R M E V O
Y W M J P L F W B X N P R I O S
A P R L W C P Y M D I E E J I V
Y P D S W E P X Y Y K K J D N U
N A I F Z O J N W L C I P S V Q
E R A Y R E P R A H M S U B R Z
M N Z Q E W U W F V V T N W S P
```

Nannie Burroughs	Mary Pleasant	Nina M.McKinley
Mary Church Terrell	Ella P. Stewart	Dr. Susan Steward
Mary Eliza Mahoney	Bessie Coleman	Ida B. Wells Barnett
Madame C.J. Walker	Harriet Tubman	Frances E. Harper
Crystal Fauset	Mary Bowser	Sojourner Truth
Florence Price	Edmonia Lewis	Ellen Craft
Ida Gray	Mary Shad Cary	

How many additional names can you add to this list? Select a name from the list and write an information paper on that person.

GA1442

African American Athletes

The last names of twenty African American athletes are hidden in the puzzle below. Can you find them all? Be sure you look vertically, horizontally, backward and diagonally.

```
J R L V Z N U R V X D S G Q D H B W Y Q
D N R Q T M P K G B F X I B Z P O F Q V
H T D E Y Y R K M D G X G U T L P D J T
C M J O K I H L A Z R O J N N O I T Y M
O V G R C D O X S R K A A M Q D O P H I
O S H E L L Q W H I C N L G D U E K C T
Q B W N R W K E E K S P H L H R F C T L
Y P T Y W V D S S N A M E R O F V F S K
J F J O R R I O K J S L T B L P T Y E Y
D T O J I B N N O S P M I S Y J E U R F
N D E U T U H R G A N N H I F D P R V Z
S Z H K R T D S U A S X W W I S H L R J
F I M R L A A K H O A R H E E E I N L Y
T H D Y N H V D N U A B X L L I T V A L
B Z I T W H I B U I Q M C G D A J U O A
C V N U C Z S K C O R I Y G Q M A X Y S
```

Evander Holyfield	Frank Robinson	George Foreman
Fritz Pollard	Reggie Jackson	O.J. Simpson
Wilma Rudolph	Julius Erving	Florence G. Joyner
Michael Jordan	Eldrick Woods	Willie Davis
Carl Lewis	Bill White	Art Shell
William Perry	Jesse Owens	Jim Rice
Arthur Ashe	Muhammad Ali	

How many additional names can you add to this list? Select a name from the list and write an information paper on that person.

GA1442

African American Educators

The last names of twenty African American educators are hidden in the puzzle below. Can you find them all? Be sure you look vertically, horizontally, backward and diagonally.

```
C G Z K Z I Y O F R E G B V B T E N
O O G Y I I X D U B O I S X M X X R
T L L K R E T B J S E O K J O Z O M
V M L L E I W J M T H T K U F E R R
J X Q V I N T A A W E R H D J I C O
W Y X U Z N O S H K L C V U A Q T R
S C Q P A W S S C M L L H T N A K G
Y Y Q W R R B O N J I A D I S E N K
U R C V F U L L A H S R L N T A U S
Y H D T G N A E Q J O K T V B H S X
L L Z Z W O O D S O N J G R H U N J
V C L G A A A T W A S H I N G T O N
V Q E S Y R K R R E Y T A V B L Q G
G B W M K B Z F I O A Z R S L C O G
C U E L R J Z Z L J M V C D R D T N
M S A I B F B N E P O H E V Q Y M E
I L T D Z K L V S Y G J Y R L M V K
```

Booker T. Washington	John H. Franklin	Nolen Ellison
Carter Woodson	Benjamin Quarles	Charles Johnson
E. Franklin Frazier	Mary M. Bethune	Marva Collins
W.E.B. Du Bois	Robert Weaver	James Nabrit
Robert Morton	Quiester Craig	Wilson Riles
Alain Locke	Kenneth Clark	Ida D. Dark
Benjamin Mays	John Hope	

How many additional names can you add to this list? Select a name from the list and write an information paper on that person.

African Americans in Government

The last names of twenty African Americans in government are hidden in the puzzle below. Can you find them all? Be sure you look vertically, horizontally, backward and diagonally.

```
C E Y J F J S J D Z P J B P L L S B F R D
A U D D S O U Z I Y P O E R Z Y U P H K P
V S M M F N P U I Z U U C W U N E M D W K
N U L Y P G O V L C K C T Y C C E E T R L
N Q F G V E O E D X C D S H W H E I E K E
S K S T H K J J W E A V E R X B J I Q A O
A Z U K X J V T I L B R I K D H L H B K U
X N H G E J H L L A H S R A M A V E B Q I
I Z P D Z Q V E C A C M P T V S W H T P U
Z J V X H T W O T H N D E U R T N S P C D
B Y U J C O I C S L I P D J B I M B O K L
F T W D P U H H E N P S V Q R E Y R B N H
W D V E U E Q S K L P L H N A D R O J R O
N A W O R T G I O Q X E X O D I E O U L S
I J Q Q K N N R T D W V B C L M D K K N F
U D I G G S J R S E P E Z L E M L E Y A G
B U H I N V I A Q K X R J S Y H I G Y X U
B N Q T I D U H Q Q J D X M P S W I R Z W
D N D M S F D K U E X B R H E N T R K F M
```

P.B.S. Pinchback
Francois Duvalier
Thomas Bradley
William Dawson
Hiram Revels
Barbara Jordan
Douglas Wilder
Carl Rowan
Oscar Dunn

Thurgood Marshall
Shirley Chisholm
David Dinkins
Ralph Bunche
Adam Powell
Patricia Harris
Charles Diggs
Andrew Young
Oscar DePriest

Richard Hatcher
Robert Weaver
Carl Stokes
William Hastie
Edward Brooke
John Lynch
Blanche Kelso Bruce

How many additional names can you add to this list? Select a name from the list and write an information paper on that person.

GA1442

African American Writers

The last names of twenty African American writers are hidden in the puzzle below. Can you find them all? Be sure you look vertically, horizontally, backward and diagonally.

```
C N Z S I T P T F Q E U J T V O B E Y N
R E K L A W V U X T G N O S L I W R M D
T L L F M C T O Z G E V H R W I R O Z Z
U L I L M L A Q R R A B N U D E A Z D D
Q U U A I J Y Z J L I T S I B O N C F E
K C F X J S L T L W V N O S W S B B Q A
K C Y H K M O R R I S O N W A D K F L U
C Y K O D E R N H F W A S A X O L J O D
S F O N T T U N S E H C U B V N X A Y S
Z R S R Z I O N C A E A O P G O M Y B H
B S G V A Q D K M C A N L F L T I N A W
L Z M D L X O I O L T Z E E V S H G R Y
Z I Y U A S L R T E L E G Z Y R U I A W
J O H M B T C E M A E F N R J U G L K L
V U M L O Q I P N V Y E A N E H H M A N
L E Z N A O S R K E Y P G J T T E T M M
G M M Z M C K A Y R R M V H F K S F C A
H C G J E G S H O A T E Z Y H B O T E C
```

Lorraine Hansberry	Toni Morrison	Nikki Giovanni
Phyllis Wheatley	Virginia Hamilton	Maya Angelou
Arna Bontemps	Zora Hurston	Eldridge Cleaver
James Johnson	Ralph Ellison	August Wilson
James Baldwin	Alice Walker	Richard Wright
Imamu Baraka	Mildred Taylor	Paul Dunbar
Langston Hughes	Frances Harper	Claude McKay
Countee Cullen	Gwendolyn Brooks	
Alex Haley	Charles Chesnutt	

How many additional names can you add to this list? Select a name from the list and write an information paper on that person.

GA1442

Answer Key

Search and Find, page 48

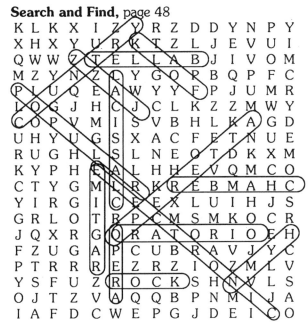

```
K L K X I Z Y R Z D D Y N P Y
X H X Y U R K T Z L J E V U I
Q W W Z T E L L A B J I V O M
M Z Y N Z L Y G O P B Q P F C
P L U Q E A W Y Y F P J U M R
L O G J H C J C L K Z Z M W Y
C O P V M I S V B H L K A G D
U H Y U G S X A C F E T N U E
R U G H L S L N E O T D K X M
K Y P H E A L H H E V Q M C O
C T Y G M L R K R E B M A H C
Y I R G I C E X L U I H J S
G R L O T R P C M S M K O C R
J Q X R G O R A T O R I O E H
F Z U G A P C U B R A V J Y C
P T R R R E Z R Z I O Z M L V
Y S F U Z R O C K S H N V L S
O J T Z V A Q Q B P N M J J A
I A F D C W E P G J D E I C O
```

Code 1, page 65

1. Stevie Wonder is a musicial genius. 2. "Finger-tips" was his first hit. 3. His mother encouraged him. 4. Success has not spoiled him. 5. He inspires other handicapped persons.

Name Dropper, page 67

1. Bessie, 2. Fats 3. Thelonious, 4. Lionel, 5. Mahalia, 6. W.C., 7. Scott, 8. Dizzy, 9. Ella, 10. Duke, 11. Miles, 12. Natalie, 13. Count, 14. Whitney, 15. Luther, 16. Patti, 17. M.C., 18. Michael, 19. Aretha, 20. Stevie, 21. Lionel, 22. Stephanie, 23. Chuck, 24. Chubby, 25. Anita

A Proclamation, page 93

1. January 1, 1863

2. Arkansas, Texas, Louisiana, Mississippi, Alabama, Florida, Georgia, South Carolina, North Carolina and Virginia

3. By the executive government of the United States, including the military and naval authorities

4. Such persons of suitable conditions will be received into the armed service of the United States. . . .

We're #1, page 105

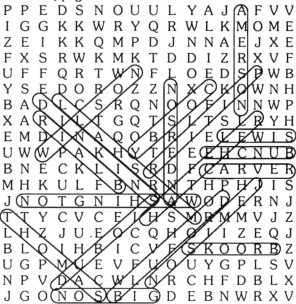

```
P P E D S N O U U L Y A J A F V V
I G G K K W R Y Q R W L K M O M E
Z E I K K Q M P D J N N A E J X E
F X S R W K M K T D D I Z R X V F
U F F Q R T W N F L O E D S P W B
Y S E D O R O Z Z N X C K O W N H
B A D L C S R Q N O O F N N N W P
X A R I L T G Q T S L T S R Y H
E M D A Q O B R I E L E W I S
U W W P A K H Y T E C H C N U B
B N E C K L I S R D F C A R V E R
M H K U L F B N R N H P H J I S
J N O T G N I H S A W O E R N J
T T Y C V C E H S M M M V J Z
L H Z J U E O C Q H Q I I Z E Q J
B L O I H B I C V F S K O O R B Z
U G P M E V F U O U Y G P L S L
N P V D A C W L N R C H F D B L X
J G O N O S B I G D E B N W R V
```

Tribute, page 110

1. The Music Award, 2. The Jackie Robinson Award, 3. The Dramatic Arts Award, 4. The Religion Award, 5. The Fine Arts Award

Movie Words, page 116

```
A J P W R M Z A C T R E S S U U J C J V H
L Q X T I E D U B B I N G D N L R B V K V
I K J B C R S O P J Q O A O C Z E T T N B
Q E K I V V D O J U H U A L A H R D M P
I C T I M D D C P I T P V Z Z U P G M L K
N P H N S M F I L M R O T I D E A Q W V E
B N K G D X Z H L Y O R R G Y H R N W H K
U Y Z Y A L P N E E R C S Y N M G R S V O
Y M S M W B U O O I I E B S E S N R
M P J W C Y Y T O A N M M A R O U C A P E
R E M R O F R E P Q O A R T U A O H G N
P Z I J T J S R U R C R T X V M R O E G
D T L E G O T C O J K E F X G T E D H I
S H R Z A I P R P T S A C E W T N I S K
Q G T J C S H I E F N O I T A M I N A E
T P S K W U O P R E T T I R W P C G H L
K Z D U O M E T R E C U D O R P S U C E
U M C J G D T F Y P A A I L F Z U E K R J
J T K Z F M Q V X H A X U R A R E M A C N
```

Back to the Future, page 120

1. Garrett Morgan, 2. George Washington Carver, 3. Ronald McNair, 4. Bill Pickett, 5. Jean Baptiste Point Du Sable, 6. Benjamin Banneker, 7. Daniel Hale Williams, 8. Matthew Henson, 9. Percy Julian, 10. James Weldon Johnson

Fact or Opinion? page 124

1. O, 2. F, 3. F, 4. O, 5. F

GA1442

Scientists and Inventors, page 126

```
U F W Y C N J B T I S T E J R B K T
A A S V S U G H U W P T B H T C D Y
Z C T Z W O G E E A B A B E R E B G
O A J U L I A N B J W E G J Y J W W
B Q N Y R U K N T J L L Q F E L I Y
E X K W D E T T D X T V G M K M R J
H T L W O P K I A W K R I A C X M S
B P S S E R Q E Q W J S O H C B T
Z L Y Y L Y B Q N F O W D M K S O P
V U V T F O R T E N L C H O K J B Y
W E R E G I L E Z T A M D B O V L D
Q U X U E I L L I R T B R N G W B Q
K H O L O P L P R E I G E B V L D A
L L K O M Z S U Q V M S W E P W M X
D R A E B O T X R R E P J J G P A J
D P T C U H R W L A R L H X O I N U
J C N V E K O G L C B U N D H R U O
J T I R M F Q W A D E Q M H G X J G
M R S V R L Y H H N P Y P F T E S P
```

Civil Rights Leaders, page 127

```
E L C Q Y W E L M A R O M G E Y M
Z V A Z F K U V L X Z Y G H H Z K
M H B N B G Z N O K W F O H T A K S
U Q P Y Q L N B K H D U A L Y E C
N T J L H Y P C A I S N I K L I W
X Q U U O S X F M T R G O M F X L
P M L T M D H E E W O X B I K J
G P F B C E N T B L R G J N U Q P
S E N O S K C A J O A E Q N P Q
H B F Y H Q H L R R C O D S H X C
F O T I T Z R B V S H A H I W R J
N Q O N F G R E G O R Y J T I V
A V F K N U Y R M P R E M L J H N
A C I L S I E T K A B X V S P M
Q N G T Y G L D I R H V L E X P H
G Z I U Z T D J W S R Q T W Z X P
O N E M B I W G U M A M R M S B
E R L Z J E E H T I B I M A R H F
```

Abolitionists, page 128

```
Y L Y A E B T F D J H I L A A Q M B N Z
W X P V U C E M C G F F F E N Y A I G Z
I C E S N C H E M I I W A R O N O M E R
E U G A K U S L M Z Z W T O E E Y M O L
E R E L S O V N O C X F U N R O L F S I
F N N X C L E H S C V G R T P T A D R
Q C J X L L T Y J Q L J N E D I V N B
O H A L L S T E W A R T E O X T S B Y
K W S A E S S N L S I S M O R C J
X I X V T L W S N E T R O F S O E P
M U R C S S G Y Z M L W R F S C N E Q A Q
R U T G Y G T M Z L E E V E D V H U D
P G P D A U E E Y V D N X K V U O W Q
W A L K E R X R F Y P G G L Y U U W D K
F B F M C Q N C X H R M Z R S R T N Y
E B E T Q F G E L S O E B C A T K Q A
A I N B Q P I D T K R Z R C D I U X D T
F B G G X F Z B K P B F L D N K Y D X W
```

Pioneers, page 129

Entertainers, page 130

Women, page 131

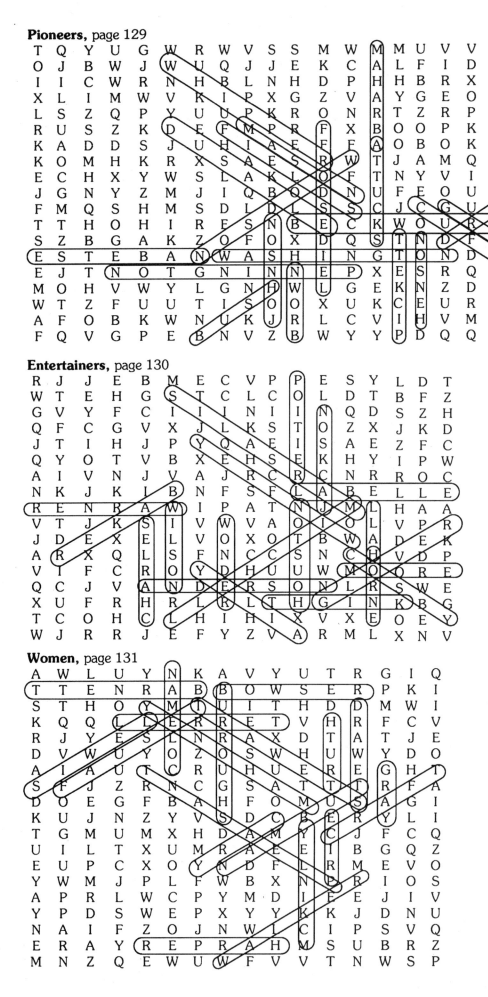

Athletes, page 132

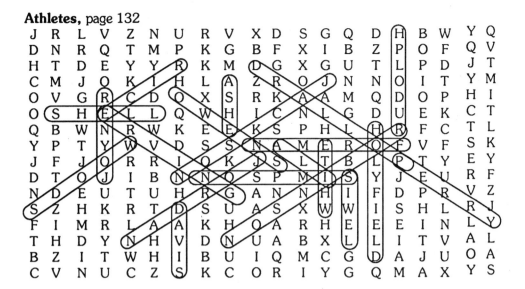

```
J R L V Z N U R V X D S G Q D H B W F Y Q
D N R Q T M P K G B F X I B Z T P O P F Q V
H T D E Y Y R K M D G X G U N N Q D J T V T
C M J O K I H L Z R O J M G O I O P K M I T
O V G R C D O X S R K A A N Q E F K C F H L
O S H E L L Q W I C N L G H R F V C F Y C T
Q B W T N R W K E K S P H L H F P T E S U S E
Y P T W V V D S N M E R O F V R F L R R
J F J Q R R I O K J L T B O L Y P U V
D T Q I B N O S P M I S J D R L
N D E U T U H R G A N N X I F S E I N A
S Z H K R L D S U S X H W E L P H J U O
F I H M R Y N H D K H O A R H X W L E I X
T H D I W H I B N U A R B C Y L A Y
B Z I U W H V S B U I Q M G Q M A S
C V N U C Z S K C O R I Y G
```

Educators, page 133

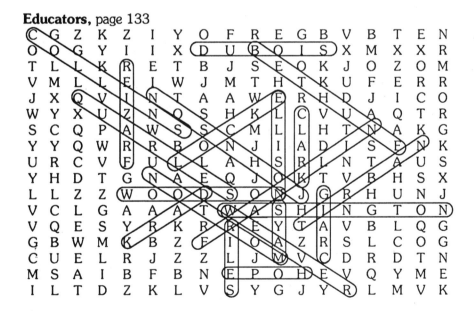

```
C G Z K Z I Y O F R E G B V B T E N
O O G Y I I X D U B O I S X M X X R N
T L L K R E T B J S E Q K J O Z O R M
V M L L E I W M T H T K U F E R R R O
J X Q I N T A A W E R H D J I C T R O
W Y X U Z N Q S H K L C V H U A Q R R G
S C Q P W S S C M L L A H T N A K K S
Y R Q W R B O N J I S C L A R I S E N G K
U Y R C V U L L A H I S L N T B U N S X J
Y H D T G N A E Q J O K T V R H U S X
L L Z Z W O O D S O N J G R H U N Q J
V C L E G A A A T W A S H I N G T O N
V Q E S Y R K R R E Y T A R B L Q G
G B W M K B Z F I O A Z R S L C O G N
C U E L R J Z Z L J M V C D R D T E
M S A I B F B N E P O H E V Q Y M E K
I L T D Z K L V S Y G J Y R L M V K
```

GA1442

Government, page 134

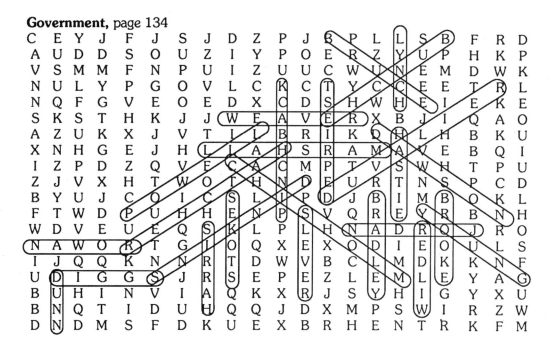

Writers, page 135

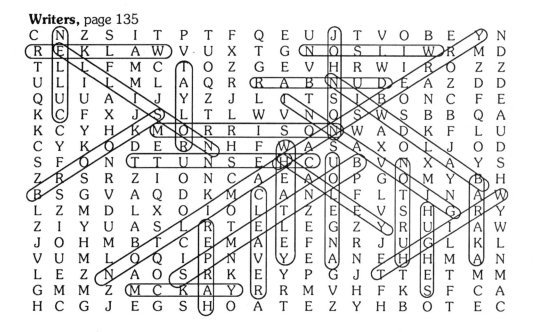

GA1442